7.00 M

To Cliff
and Angie,
Best neighbours!
Rich

Richard Cumyn

VIKING BRIDES

We acknowledge the support of the Canada Council for the Arts, the Ontario Arts Council and the Government of Canada through the Book Publishing Industry Development Program for our publishing activities.

The author is grateful to the Canada Council for the Arts and the Nova Scotia Arts Council for funding received during the creation of this book, and to the editors of the following journals, where some of these stories were first published: *The New Quarterly, Event, Cross-Connect, Fiddlehead, Prairie Fire, Blue Moon Review* and *Mississippi Review*. Thanks, with love, to my first reader, Sharon Murphy. Also many thanks to Ian Colford, Sue MacLeod, Brian Bartlett, Julie Vandervoort, Thomas Hubschman, Eleonore Schönmaier and Sylvana Buttigieg, who read early versions of the stories.

ISBN 0 7780 1177 1 (hardcover)
ISBN 0 7780 1179 8 (softcover)

ONTARIO ARTS COUNCIL
CONSEIL DES ARTS DE L'ONTARIO

Cover art by Prudence Heward
Book design by Michael Macklem

Printed in Canada

PUBLISHED IN CANADA BY OBERON PRESS

Contents

To my mother
and in memory of my father

Hodzik's of Hollywood

When Lorenc came into the showroom to say that the photographer was threatening to leave, he noticed Harris Noonan standing between the baby-doll nighties and the camisoles, his bicycle helmet upturned in his hands like a hopeful bowl. Lorenc nodded to him, then told his mother that his sister needed a different outfit because they could see everything.

"Lorenc!"

"That's what she said."

"What about the pink? The flounced with the matching cover-up?"

"That's the one she's wearing."

Mama was helping the only customer in the shop, a woman holding a bathing-suit clearly too small for her against her front. Lorenc didn't recognize her and knew he probably wouldn't see her in the store again. They were never from town and they rarely came back. He wondered why his father had even built the display-room as an extension of the house, a low-brow, brown bunker of a bungalow, since most of their revenue came from mail orders and from the handful of lingerie stores that carried the Hodzik line. He imagined the showroom was his father's concession to Mama for having moved her from Montreal to Clayton, this tiny village south of Ottawa. Clayton had one main street, a railway crossing, a school, two churches, a grocery store, a post office, a Tai Kwon Do school above a tanning salon, a gas station, an automated bank machine, and not much else. Although no-one they knew ever came into the showroom, it was the place where Mama conducted her social life, such as it was.

"We're not too sure about this patchwork effect," said the customer to her reflection. Lorenc glanced at the mirror. "No, we're not," said the woman's double, doubtfully.

7

"You won't know until you try it on," said Mama. "This pattern is designed to flatten any woman's figure."

The cyclist shifted his feet, the stiff-soled black shoes scuffing on the tile. He cleared his throat nervously.

"You mean *flatter*, I think, Mama," said Lorenc.

"I think this gentleman requires assistance," she replied, her dark eyes flashing her annoyance.

"That's no gentleman, that's Harris." Lorenc basked in the bright pink glow of the boy's face.

Harris Noonan was one of those placid, gangly, earnest, pizza-faced boys who show their prize heifers and sows at 4H competitions, and who grow up to sit on the board of directors of the feed and seed co-op and help organize the fall agricultural fair. Lorenc knew the reason why Harris was standing here treading water in a lingerie lagoon.

As if conjured by her brother, Catriona Hodzik swept into the room through the doorway connecting the show-room to the house. She had draped around her a man's large, green-and-red plaid dressing gown that she held closed with one hand at the neck. She made directly for her mother, who was stout and matronly in a long-sleeved, navy dress, yet graced with Catriona's full pouty lips and amber eyes. The girl kept her eyes lowered as she bent at the waist to bring her mouth close to the woman's ear.

"I know, I know, Catya," she soothed, "this is the last time, I promise." She hugged her daughter to her breast and stroked her hair. "What about the Widow Maker, the black with the little skirt in front? It's quite respectable."

Catriona covered her eyes with her hand.

"Where can I try this on?" asked the woman holding the bathing suit.

Lorenc showed her to the dressing-room, an empty closet with a ceiling light, chair and curtain for a door.

Outside the window that looked onto the regional road, the one that became Main Street once it hit the Clayton town line, a man carrying a parabolic light reflector and its tripod stand walked hurriedly by. An ominous rip came from the change-room.

"Dragan! He's leaving. Don't let him go before he's finished," cried Mama.

"He's finished," her husband yelled back from inside the house. "We're all finished with him. Lorenc, my camera, please, get it from my bedroom closet. The world is hostage to imbeciles who charge $40 the hour to pick their noses!"

Lycra, nylon, polyester, latex; straps, harnesses, girdles, clips, Velcro fasteners; lace patterns, leopard spots, snake-skin and zebra stripes; orange, black, tan, nude, red, pink, purple; shiny, transparent, feathered, furred: every guise imaginable for the female body, second skins, theatre marquees and carnival barkers for the first. In the midst of it, two innocents: a mud-splattered boy in tight black bicycling shorts and zippered jersey, and his Venus de Milo, blushing, draped in the least feminine and, to the cyclist Harris Noonan, the most surprisingly suggestive of fabrics. Wearily Catriona dipped her hand into the pocket of the gown, took out a pair of black-framed glasses, put them on, and tucked her hair, which matched the colour of the frames, behind her ears.

The photographer's car pulled out of the driveway and disappeared. The woman in the change-room emerged non-chalantly and sidled empty-handed out of the showroom. Lorenc retrieved the *maillot*, took it through to the room where the women sat working at sewing machines, and he gave it to Lana, who was too bright for this kind of work. He thought she should be giving guided tours of the Parliament Buildings or reporting the five-day forecast on the Weather Channel or drawing up business plans for people like his father. She interpreted for the group, kept the other six on-task, corrected their mistakes, and intervened between them and Hodzik whenever he was an unpredictable gale bringing them yet another crude sketch to turn into a workable design.

9

Her fingers scouted the edges of the rip, and she shook her head slightly. It was a bad design. Hodzik wouldn't let them use the necessary lining and finished double-stitch that such a garment demanded. She looked up at Lorenc to let him know that nothing could be done about it, and stuffed the *maillot* into her handbag at her feet. Lorenc knew that she would rather work late into the night making a replacement at her kitchen table than risk letting his father find the ripped one lying in the trash bin.

Some mornings Lorenc wished that the seamstresses would not be waiting in the liquor store parking-lot on Somerset West when he drove up, that they would have disappeared, and that his father would have to do something else for a living: be a baker or a berry farmer or a market gardener. The family could open a Hungarian restaurant like the one his Uncle Laszlo managed in downtown Ottawa in the Byward Market. They could rent space in the new strip mall out by the badge-spattered Lion's Club sign welcoming people into town. His father would not have to do a thing. Mama could greet their patrons as they came in, and each person would be beaming to see the Hodziks engaged, finally, in a respectable endeavour. Catriona could serve, Lorenc could cook, they would find someone to wash dishes, and eventually the business would be doing well enough that they could hire another waiter or two. All their neighbours, everyone in town would come and know them by name and praise the food, the fine wine, the music, the soothing décor. Catriona would no longer feel she had to hide her face. They could have friends over to the house, be invited to other homes. Catriona could get herself gone.

Many a boy, intrigued by the seductive image Catriona presented in the advertisements and the yearly mail-order catalogue, had tried unsuccessfully to ask her out to parties and dances. Each one was put off by the contrast between the allure of the photographs and the excruciating reticence of the real girl, who always declined the invitation in a timorous whisper. If one of them knocked at the door and asked to see Catriona, and if his tone had even a hint of mockery in it, he was rebuffed by Mama's silent, withering stare or by her husband's harrowing scrutiny. Or, if a boy telephoned and sounded sincere, he might be invited to supper without ever having been allowed to speak with the object of his desire. Only one had ever accepted the invitation and he left to go home halfway through the meal.

Nevertheless there was one who fell smack flat for Catriona, ungracefully, misplacing his head in the very thicket of love. The boy, the same Harris Noonan who waited patiently in the showroom for her now, would watch for her in the halls between classes, and sit across from her in the cafeteria at lunch-time. Since he never made overt demands on her affection, she didn't have to reject him, but neither did she encourage him. She managed to uncave her shoulders whenever he was near, lift her chin a degree or two higher than usual. Lorenc, big brother, kept a watchful distance.

Harris once copied out a published poem and slipped it into Catriona's locker, leaving a corner of the white page showing. Lorenc took it out before his sister could notice it. At first he couldn't see why Harris had done this, for it hardly seemed a love poem. Perhaps it was something for English class. Then, re-reading the carefully printed poem on lined foolscap, all about the sensual delights of eels and mussels prepared in sauces that ravished the taste buds, releasing the deepest magic of the sea, he understood what the poet was saying to his unnamed love, and knew that this meal of *Eros*, which the man would prepare for her in his adoration, was the one Harris Noonan longed to spread before Catriona Hodzik.

This particular late September morning before dawn, a Saturday, a cold fog had drifted up from the Rideau River, across the cornfields and into town. The fog blanketed the ground to the top of the company van. Lorenc was suddenly awake to it enveloping the vehicle. It was as if the engine started *him* each morning, and he had to think: had he really awakened to the alarm clock's bleat, gotten dressed in the dark, left the house like a burglar, shoes in hand, to find himself sitting here in darkness and gauze, the ignition key vibrating between his thumb and forefinger?

He slid off the driver's seat, left the door of the van swung open, and quietly unhooked the wire barrier and sign—*Private Property / Hodzik Closed Please*—strung across the entrance to the driveway. He needn't have been so stealthy: his father was awake and having the first of a dozen cups of black coffee he would consume in a day, and his mother was busy removing the plastic dustcovers from the sewing machines. They knew where he was going each morning in the dark night before school. Only Catriona was still asleep, and neither the sound of the coffee grinder nor the van's engine ever woke her.

The road out of Clayton ran east, past the blue strip-mall in its last stages of construction, past the garbage dump now full and closed, past two large dairy farms, one belonging to the Van Peldts and the other to Lester Jacobsen, Dick Van Peldt's son-in-law, whose idea it had been to build an indoor golf driving range. Mr. Van Peldt ran with the idea, buying the old municipal drill hall, a corrugated steel building that looked like an aircraft hangar, when it came to be replaced by a new community centre, and reconstructing the metal shell on his property. His wife threatened to leave him over it, their existing barns one strong wind away from collapse, but he had stubbornly stuck to his dream, counting on the winter revenue from grateful, snowbound golfers to build him three new barns before the old ones could squash his Holsteins. And he was right. Five years later he had handsome new quarters for the cows, and the golf enterprise made almost as much as the farm did, having been expanded to include an outdoor range, a mini-putt course, and a nine-hole par-27.

The road ended near Van Peldt's, meeting a similar one that ran north along the route stagecoaches used to follow. A few timber and stone houses, former wayfarers' inns, were still standing. After the railway was built and the roads paved for cars, the inns and way stations went out of business, and were left to crumble at the side of the road or sold to people who moved out from the city and into the sturdy structures distinguished by a single dormer window set in a sharp peak above the entrance. Lorenc dreamed of sleeping in a room with a window like that, in a bed set under the tent the dormer's roof made of the ceiling. He would be Lorenc in the Attic, in a venerable house made of no synthetic material. He could turn it back into an inn. It could house their five-star dining-room.

The sky grew lighter and he felt the city's flavour growing stronger as he drove, past the harness-racing track where some of his classmates worked after school and on weekends, past the last drive-in theatre in the region, past a gravel pit and the warehouses of a business park. In another twenty minutes he was in the west end of the city, where Clayton Township, its pungent fields as foreign as the Russian steppes, was unknown. Here were brick buildings in blocks crowded together and marred by cryptic spray-painted script, greasy storefront windows streaked with condensation, dented metal garbage cans. Nothing here was green-leafed, no vista unhemmed.

When Lorenc arrived at the parking-lot of the liquor store, a black-and-white police van sat canted at curb-side, its right-hand wheels resting on the sidewalk, its top light flashing. Two policemen burdened with bulky vests and leather at the hip dwarfed Lana, the group's spokeswoman, as they listened to her. He wondered if she would be considered the comeliest of the group back in her country. He tried to picture her wearing a lace teddy, but couldn't.

He eased the van past them without slowing or turning

his head to look, hoping none would give a sign of recognition. He did not know what to do. If he arrived home without the seamstresses, his father would shout and break things and make Lorenc owe him the day's lost productivity. Catriona would have to stay home from school to help their mother sew. Cat's eyes would sting by the end of the day and Mama would have to soak her stiff fingers in warm water and salts.

He turned the corner and stopped at a parking-meter, turned off the engine, felt his thoughts halt along with it. It was still well before the time when he would have to put coins in the meter. How long should he wait? Five minutes—no, ten, he decided, then he would get out and walk back toward the pick-up spot. If the women were still there and the police were gone, he would tell them to meet him somewhere else, perhaps at two or three spots removed from each other. He should have been doing this all along. Hadn't his father told him to make several stops and to vary the rendezvous places from time to time? The women hardly spoke English, and once the liquor store had been agreed upon, it became convenient for all to meet there.

When he rounded the corner he saw with relief that the paddy wagon was gone and the women, looking like a flock of sparrows on the verge of flight, were still there. He raised his hand in greeting, but from a distance and without the van to identify him, he was just another of the tall, menacing, white youths the women had learned to avoid. They moved closer together, eyeing him uneasily until he came close enough to be recognized, and then they rushed him, speaking quickly and all at once in a mixture of English and Spanish and Tagalog.

It came out, haltingly, that the police had asked them many questions: Who were they? Where did they live? Where were they going? What were they doing out so early in the morning? Lana said that she had already thought of a story to tell in just such a circumstance. The others subsided and let her tell it, nodding their heads and smiling to mask their apprehension. She said that she told the police they were waiting for a shuttle bus to take them to the airport. She said they were a visiting badminton team from Manila and were waiting for their coach to pick them up. Where was all their equipment? The coach had it. Were they late? Could the police help them get to the airport on time? No, their coach was always on time. What were they doing in this neighbourhood? the police had asked, indicating the run-down tenements and the absence of hotels in the vicinity. Where had they stayed the night? To save money, Lana explained, they had slept in the apartment of a relative. It had been quite comfortable.

"*My* cousin!" said one mischievously, bouncing slightly on her toes and beaming up at Lorenc.

"That was a close call," he said, and waited while Lana translated for the rest. He pointed to his watch and gestured for them to follow him back to the van. They hesitated. "Come," he said, "I'm parked around the corner."

"No," she said. "You drive back here, please." He was about to protest when he recognized what her unwavering eyes and folded arms were saying, that this indeed had been too close a call, that this was a furthest point for them. They would not parade after him, like ducks after bread-crumbs down the city sidewalk in the brightening light of the unfurling day, not even such a short distance.

He heard his father yell, "Lorenc! Camera!" and then his mother's pleading voice: the session was over, Catriona was tired, she had homework to do, they could use last season's pictures, let the girl get dressed. Please, Dragan, for pity's sake! The bickering continued for a few moments and stopped. Even the seamstresses stopped running their machines to listen.

Lorenc left the sewing-room and went down the hallway into the living-room with its mantelpiece photo of his father, uncle and grandfather newly arrived in Halifax. It was 1956, his father was nine years old, Laszlo, twelve. Who had taken the picture? A steerage mate, a fellow Displaced Person? Or was it an immigration officer pleased to have been given a brief respite from deciphering thickly burred accents and recording unpronounceable names? The three of them looked wan and leery but resolute: what relief, after fright, flight and fugitive seas, did this raw, unknown country hold for them, they appeared to be thinking? Whatever little, it promised more than did Budapest at that moment. Whenever Lorenc looked at the photo he felt their disapproving eyes on him: What do you know, boy, about having to start over from nothing?

He passed the closed door of his father's little office. Inside was a drafting-table, bare walls, tilting stacks of fashion magazines covering the floor, desk and window sill, and one bristly occupant whose presence made the thin walls bulge, and who emerged from under the abutments of his will to poison the wells of their slow-filling peace. Get your own camera why don't you, Lorenc wanted to write on a piece of paper and slip under the door as he might a letter bomb. He went into his parents' bedroom, rummaged through shoeboxes stacked at the back of his father's clothes closet, found the Brownie in its old leather case, and on his way back down the hall hung it by its strap over the office's door handle. He considered knocking to alert his father of its presence, but decided not to.

Harris had been standing there for so long waiting to speak to Catriona that when he did speak they were startled by his voice. They had forgotten he was there, a scarecrow suddenly given the gift of words in a meadow of many colours.

"Hullo," he croaked, his voice cracking high and then diving deep into a basement register on the second syllable, "I was wondering—"

But before he could finish his rehearsed request, that he

16

hoped Catriona was not too busy on this lovely afternoon to go for a short walk with him, perhaps along the path that connected the seniors' home to the post office and ran behind all the houses on that side of Main Street, he was cut off by the sound of a shrill whistle.

Outside was a newly arrived truck, its open back crammed with boys from the school, all of them wearing the same leather jacket: baby blue with a large fabric decal depicting the head and headdress of a Spartan soldier on the back. Eight of them in all, three from inside the cab and five vaulting over the side of the truck's bed, streamed through the door.

Lorenc recognized the boy who had been driving and two of the others, but because he never stayed after school to watch the football games, and because these boys were a year older than he was, he had little reason to know them. They fanned through the merchandise in even formation as if fresh from a broken huddle. The first practice of the year was over and there were novices to be initiated. Their arrival here, with wet hair and nervous hands, was only the first step in a sequence of events that would see the rookies exchanging their jeans and sweaters for selected pieces of the Hodzik line (paid for, it was rumoured, out of the school's physical education budget), and engaging in increasingly imaginative and depraved acts, the marathon culminating, just before dawn in the Rose Room of the Four Corners Grill and Gas Bar, with the heads of the initiates hung heavy over a toilet bowl or nestled angelically in the bosom of the local talent.

Hodzik chose that moment to shuffle into the showroom. His jowls were covered by a nap of white and black bristle, two-days' worth. Bifocals slid almost to the tip of a strong nose and his chin hugged his throat as he sighted through the viewfinder of the camera. His black mop of hair was tinged with ash. He wore a stained blue workshirt with buttoned pockets, trousers the same colour but a shade darker, and shabby bedroom slippers.

"We have no film, Lorenc," he said in a voice too small and distant for him, distracted as he was by the tiny image of people and underwear hanging upside down from the ceiling. Lorenc thought he heard his father release a low growl from the back of his throat, the man realizing perhaps that it was that day in autumn again when his wares, and by association he, became objects of derision.

"You know what we need, Lorry," he said quietly, his words small in the sudden stillness of the room, as he halted and then retraced his steps backwards, still fixed on the inverted square at his chest.

Lorenc was relieved to see his father retreat this time; there had been the year when Hodzik had thrown the interlopers out of the store for their impudence only to have someone return in the night to back a tanker truck onto the lot and spray liquid pig manure over the windows of the house and van. Lorenc sensed something different in the demeanour of the Spartan warriors this time. They looked preoccupied, too studious of the flimsy garments, not raucous enough. They were standing and inspecting things the way a father will stand in a clothing store for young women while his teenage daughter tries on a new outfit for a school dance.

"How may I help you, gentlemen?" said Mama, her voice an anvil wrapped in velvet.

All the players' eyes shifted to focus on the driver, the architect of this year's lark, who produced a copy of the previous season's Hodzik catalogue from a pocket sewn into the lining of his team jacket. Magician, thought Lorenc, quarterback, politician, square-head, big-necked bagman, farm boy of fun. He felt the boy's sweaty fingers staining Catriona's portrait on the cover.

"We were wondering, ma'am, if this—if your model here," and he held up the catalogue, "might be available for a private function."

"And what do you mean by 'available,' sir?" said Mama.

"Well, that depends totally, you know, on her. We're willing to pay the going rate. I mean, like, we got a good size budget and all."

Mama moved closer to the boy and fixed her eyes intently on his.

"How much money?"

Lorenc felt his stomach lurch. "Mama."

"I'm discussing business with this nice young...businessman. Now, continue."

"We were thinking of like a fashion show? She could model some of the outfits here. We're talking, I don't know, forty-five minutes, an hour tops? Hundred bucks."

"A hundred dollars? For an hour's work?" The way Mama moved her head from side to side, keeping a lock on the boy's eyes, reminded Lorenc of a cobra swaying in front of its prey. Catriona let out a despairing groan.

"This is ridiculous, Mama. You don't know what they want her to do." The gang turned a collective look of contempt on him.

"They want her to model some clothes. Don't you? What is your name, by the way?" He told her. "Vince. Vincent, like the painter. A fine name. What love will make a man do, eh, Vincent? That's all you require, is it not? A fashion show? You aren't suggesting anything you might be ashamed of, are you? My Catriona is a beautiful girl. You see it, don't you? That's what drew you here, not the garments but the living person. Admit it. Go ahead, you can say it. You are a little bit falling in love with her, just from her picture, and all this time you haven't even noticed her standing right behind me. She breathes."

"I'm going to my room, Mama," said Catriona, but she stayed still.

The boy stammered something indistinct that had the tone of a denial, but was cut off by Mr. Hodzik's bellow.

"Are they gone yet?"

"It's all right, Dragan, go back to what you were doing!

"My husband. Did you know that he designs every one of these garments?" One of the boys snickered as Mama swept her arm in a theatrical arc. She swivelled her head and locked onto the offender, silencing him. "He is an artist himself, you know, a man of immense talent. He takes great pride in these creations, all of them made to honour the female body. Do you know why he uses his own daughter instead of a stranger to pose for these pictures? The reason is this simple: he has her in his mind's eye for every design. That is why they are of the greatest beauty. The line, the colour, the drape and texture of them. That is what drew you here, isn't it? You can admit that, can't you, Vincent. You are a man, after all, no longer a little boy. You appreciate the finer things."

"Alls we want is a fuckin' stripper, for fuck sake," came a slurred voice.

Vincent the quarterback rolled his eyes.

When they left, sheepishly, each of the warriors went out with a purchase in hand—"for your mother or your girl-friend," suggested Mrs. Hodzik—something suitably full-length, long-sleeved, cotton-blend and opaque.

She turned to Harris, "Now, sir, how may I help you? An intimate gift for someone special?"

Harris, unable to articulate his desire, the blood in his ears deafening, stood mute.

"We're all going out, the three of us," said Lorenc, who could feel alarm from each of them, mother, sister, tongue-tied suitor, he himself. "It's all right, isn't it, Mama? Just for a little while? We thought we'd go somewhere. You know. Not for too long."

Where? Where? Think!

"To...Van Peldt's. To hit a bucket of balls." He dared not look at either of them for fear of losing his resolve.

She said absolutely not, then no, then perhaps, and fi-nally gave her consent, promising to hold her husband at bay but only for a couple of hours. "You're not back by supper-time, I can't be held responsible."

Both Harris and Catriona were blushing. Lorenc broke the spell by urging her to go and dress, which she did, quickly, and when she climbed into the van, where the boys were already waiting, she was wearing sneakers, a pair of baggy jeans and a faded sweatshirt. She had removed her makeup and looked so fit and eager that she might have yelled or sung a song if there had been a need to do so.

Lorenc drove them to the range, rented two number-2 woods and two buckets of yellow balls, and was content to sit on a bench and watch him tutor her in the rudiments of making square contact between club face and ball. Harris was a good teacher, patient, encouraging, able to break the motion of the swing into a sequence of natural frames. As he stood behind her with his arms over top of hers to help adjust her grip, she didn't shrink at his touch, but moved back so that she was in contact with his chest. All along the row of rubber-matted tees lining one side of the building came the random, explosive sounds followed by the sigh of the nylon netting accepting the projectiles and dropping them to the dirt. When the buckets were empty, Catriona said, "No. So soon?" in a voice so musical and tragic that the men on either side of them turned to look at her.

They took the back road home and stopped at an apple orchard, where they bought a bag and took it to a barn that the owners had set up with cargo nets and a swinging tire for kids to play on. They climbed over the apparatus and flopped into the hay, and then just lay there crunching the hard fruit and looking up at the slivers of steel sky above the rafters.

Lorenc tossed his core away, and said it was time to go. "Don't want to anger Cronus," he said.

Catriona said that they would meet him at home. It was not a long walk from there. He hesitated, preparing to argue logic, when he stopped himself. They were holding hands. He had never seen her so firm, so sure of her direction, so ready to comply with gravity.

He returned home and then drove the seamstresses back into the city. They agreed that he would pick three of them up at Carlingwood shopping-centre and four in front of the Civic Hospital on Monday morning. When he returned, Catriona and Harris were not home yet. His mother held supper, distracting his father by sending him to Brundidge's for olive oil and the Superstore in Johnsville for dinner rolls. Finally they strolled in as if time no longer existed for them. Mr. Hodzik was unable to say anything to intimidate Harris, who spent most of the meal gazing at Catriona. She and her mother moved back and forth from the table to the stove and refrigerator, and once disappeared altogether for a few minutes, returning with looks of resolve on their faces.

Lorenc tied Harris' bike to the back of the van and drove him home. The darkness reminded Lorenc of the mornings before school, driving into the city before anyone else was awake. The boys said thanks and you're welcome and see you around. Harris said what a good meal it had been, as good as anything he had eaten in a restaurant, and Lorenc said yes, it sure had. It was something they would do again, he said. Soon, soon, not soon enough.

"Catriona's not going to pose for any more of those pictures," said Harris. "She told me that on the walk home."

"I know," said Lorenc. "I mean, it doesn't surprise me," but inside he was sprinting on his toes, thrusting his arms into the clouds, tearing through drywall with a crowbar to expose smiling stone walls, all the while wondering how one went about cooking an eel and where, where in this cowshit pasture by a sluggard river did one acquire anything as immense and flirtatious as a mussel.

Drainage

This year almost everyone had reason to stay late: Angela Benson slapped one of her students in early November and was transferred to the board office; Gordon Minnes' wife was now two years home from *her* teaching job without having made much progress getting off the living-room couch; the new drama teacher, Joel Sadinsky, let some of his students go into the fields behind the school on their snowmobiles to videotape their own version of *Macbeth*, and one of the boys fell off and broke his back. Rob Morris from science took up with Linda Sampson from modern languages, and they extinguished their marriages and their affair in barely more time than it took to compose, administer and mark their January exams. Dave Semple was accused of calling the only black student in the school, Byron Day, lazy during a post-exam interview in which Byron questioned his failing mark and suggested that racial prejudice was the reason for the low grade. Indira Basu from Student Services summoned Semple to her office, where she recounted what she had heard from the boy, who was in tears by the time he got to her, and she asked icily if he might not have said something the boy mistook for something else. Dave insisted he told Byron only that the boy could work harder at the subject, Grade 12 math. Byron's father, Lanford Day, a long-standing township councillor, prosperous realtor and former provincial track star, threatened legal action on his son's behalf, but nothing came of it. In April the teachers went on strike against the board of education, and while they were walking the picket line Byron Day drove his car into a tree and died.

That sort of thing.

Dave was the first to arrive. He asked what needed to be done. Rob told him to break up a block of ice into a washtub and pack it with bottles of beer. The pool, glinting in the strong sun, looked like a window of blue ice surrounded by burlap. Trees were something Rob was getting around to. A steel-link fence separated his crisp lawn from the cornfield behind and on either side of the house. They sat in recliners at the shallow end of the pool.

Rob tipped half the contents of a beer down his throat, and then used the neck of the bottle to point at a spot beyond the fence.

"Every year I make my senior chemistry class test their well water. Guess how many different chemicals they find."

"I don't know. Twelve."

"You're way off. Try again."

"I have no idea, Rob. How many?"

"Dozens, a full page single-spaced. And we aren't even set up to test for the really exotic ones. All the heavy metals: lead, cadmium, mercury. PCBs, ketone, carbon tetrachloride—dry-cleaning solvent, Dave! All the way out here. Gasoline, pesticides. We're still finding DDT. Formaldehyde. These are just defenceless sand-point wells."

"Have you had yours tested?" asked Dave.

Rob looked at him and laughed. It said, 'If you want to think about it, go ahead. To you I pass the mantle of worry.'

Rob confessed that he had been drinking since before the previous day's graduation ceremony. Neither teacher had made it to the staff brunch at the Strudel Haus. Dave had awakened cold and muddled in a field beside the smouldering remains of the grads' bonfire; since the day the strike ended, Rob was unable to fall asleep until after dawn.

A woman Dave didn't know came out and stood between their chairs. She had a healthy glass in one hand and car keys in the other. Rob asked her what she was drinking and she said gin and lime. He introduced her as Clarisse.

"I'm going to buy more burgers," she said. "I don't think you have enough. Can you think of anything else?"

"Mix," he said. "We'll run out in the first hour on a day

24

like this."

After she had gone back into the house, he yelled, "Round up some more chairs, will you! Clarisse! Are you there?"

He told Dave that Clarisse was a neighbour who had helped Rob's wife, Dawn, with the kids during the time when Rob had moved in with Linda Sampson. Dawn kept seeing Clarisse in the same places she went: the hockey arena, the grocery store, fairs and concerts at the public school. Their children, three each, paired into similar age slots.

Rob thought Clarisse was fonder of the house and its scent of recent scandal than she was of slighted Dawn and her abandoned children, and when Dawn finally took the kids away for good to her parents' home in Thunder Bay, Clarisse didn't see any reason to be a stranger. It was a bigger house than hers. The washer and dryer worked. Rob had a satellite dish and was always well stocked with liquor. Her kids appreciated the pool, the eldest, Frank, proclaiming he would be the cabana boy for $50 a month. Rob told him, "You, Francis Chiarelli, are a piratical operator."

Frank had done a lovely job cleaning the pool. He was not there today, Rob explained, because he was in the city with his father, but his sisters were around somewhere.

"Janine! Come out and meet Dave. Janine!" No-one answered. "Shouldn't people be arriving already? The thing should be over by now."

Dave agreed that it was strange that no-one else from the school was there yet. Some years the staff brunch and the pool party had been held at the same place so that people could start early to yelp and splash and dance, knocking loose the cotter pins holding them to the last ten months.

"Did you bring your bathing-suit? You look like you slept on the ground last night."

"I did," said Dave. "And I did."

"Fool."

25

He changed in a grimy downstairs bathroom. Wet towels were mounded on the floor, the back of the toilet, the bottom of the bathtub. He came out, put the rolled bundle of his shirt, trousers and underwear beside his shoes and socks under his chair, and let himself fall backwards into the water. When he stood up, bits of grass were floating around him. He tried to scoop them up with cupped hands. Rob handed him a long-handled net and a freshly opened beer. Dave climbed out and began working the net one-handed down the length of one side of the pool. He let the brilliance of the water blind him before shutting his eyes tightly. His shoulders and back dried instantly. He moved in a bubble of good cheer.

"You can fire Franky," he said, "I'm taking over. No more polynomials. No more side-angle-side."

"Did you get your marks in?" asked Rob.

It was an odd question. They had each taught graduating classes that year. Dave hesitated before saying, "You haven't yet?"

"Haven't even looked at their finals. The piles are in there somewhere. I offered Clarisse money to mark them, but she just laughed at me."

"What's on their transcript, then?"

"January marks, I guess. Who knows? I told them it wasn't going to get done, not by me, not anytime soon."

Knowing this made Dave feel disoriented. For all the times he had coasted, skimping on a lesson, pulling ready-made practice sheets out of his files, he had always marked everything and had never missed the deadline to submit grades for the report card.

"You think I'm a bum," said Rob.

"I'm not saying that."

"I'm considering a year off, getting into another line. Maybe bus tours. Science field trips and that."

Dave said that sounded like a good idea.

A girl ran out and cannon-balled into the pool directly in

front of where Dave was standing, sending a drenching spray over him. She stood knee-deep, smiling up at him. She had the concave, rubber spine of childhood, fawn's legs, high haunches stuck on as an afterthought, a superfluous bikini top.

"Janine makes her entrance. Where's your sister?"

"Under your bed," she said, before committing a hand-stand in the water. Her legs scissored, and she toppled backwards.

Dave was beginning to feel displaced: the pool and its surroundings were in motion around him. He'd had three bottles of Rob's fortified home brew in quick succession. The direct sun was making his head tilt and slosh. He'd eaten nothing since the night before. The pool rose to meet him.

He stood and coughed for air. The water around him was tinted pink. Rob was telling him not to move. Then he said, "Get out carefully. Watch where you step. How did you manage to do that? I'll vacuum the pieces. Show him where the first-aid box is, Janine, please. Where did Frank put the attachment?"

The sensation was one of being an audience participant in a play that moved to a different location with each scene. He climbed out of the pool, stanched his hand with a towel, followed the girl into the same bathroom where he had changed into his bathing-suit, and let her clean the wound with peroxide.

"You're cut off," she said.

She opened a butterfly bandage and put it into position. It didn't feel as if there was any glass in the cut, a small but deep puncture in the fleshy part at the base of his right thumb.

"Are you feeling all right?" She repeated the question. "You should sit down."

The light in the bathroom dimmed. He sat hard on the toilet seat. His skin was clammy and twitching. He waved her out of the room and put his head between his knees. He heard the door close. Sight returned, first a grainy grey, then colours. He slid off the seat, knelt, turned and lifted the lid in what felt like a series of graceful movements. Even the gush from his throat had a focused trajectory.

When he looked in the mirror, his face was freckled with spidery red blotches Rob told him later were capillaries burst from the violence of the emesis. He felt surprisingly strong and observant.

He heard a knock on the door. "Dave, you all right in there?"

Clarisse was there when he opened, her concern gradually replaced by puzzlement at the sight of his face. She fussed, checked his cut, replaced the bandage with a bigger one even though the bleeding had stopped, banned him from the water, established him in a safe chair under a sun umbrella and gave him a glass of ginger ale to nurse.

Rob said, "Get him a hat, he needs a hat. You sure you don't want me to drive you home?"

He assured them he was fine. He'd made it to every year-end party since his first year at the school. It was more than tradition; he was superstitious about it. The summer might never come if he missed the party. He needed the excess of it, the release, the penance of recovery from it. Otherwise July and August might evaporate in a bitter stew, and September arrive like the guest no-one is prepared for.

Clarisse brought a little girl outside, and slipped orange inflatable sleeves up her arms. The woman put her lips to one of the plastic nipples, puffed her cheeks out as she blew, then stopped the hole.

"Becky, keep your hat and sunglasses on, please. No, they'll be perfectly fine if you get them wet. Yes, I can let some air out, but not too much or you won't be able to float."

Rob asked again how he was feeling, but got up before Dave answered. The sound of an approaching car came from the side of the house. The back of a green van appeared between the garage and the fence, and stopped so that its back wheels were even with the shallow end of the pool.

The driver got out, opened the rear doors of the vehicle, climbed in and reappeared rolling a metal beer keg, which Rob helped him carry into the house. The man looked familiar. Dave tried to place him. Rob introduced him: Gilles Bodoin, the music and French language teacher who had quit to raise dairy cattle the year before Dave was hired. They had met a few years before at another of these parties. Bodoin led a blues band that played the bar circuit on weekends.

He took a guitar case out of the front seat of his van, and from it lifted a steel version of the instrument. Devilishly he caught the sun and shone it into Dave's eyes before settling into a slide number.

"That a silencer on your finger or is it just glad to see me?" said Rob.

Janine's laugh said, 'Thanks, oh yes, for this naughty world.'

Her mother said, "Tell me what you find so hilarious, young lady."

Dave thought, 'Well, slide on, Gilles Bodoin, happy freed man for whom this is just the middle of a summer day, nothing special. The planting's been done for a month and the cows are sated. You have nothing but that portion the sun and the rain and the good earth deign is yours.'

The musician played, reaching through secret openings in Dave's body and replacing much that the year had taken. When he closed his eyes, colours bloomed with different notes. Gilles improvised a song about the rest of the teaching staff:

"Don't tell me they gone,
"Gone back to the zoo,
"I can drain this barrel myself, baby,

29

"But some need it more than I do.

"It been a long, long year."

Rob got his cell phone and the directory from inside, and began leafing through the book. "Even when Gilles was teaching, we needed it more than he did. I never seen such a slack-ass operation as the one he had going in that band-room. He'd give the baton to the class keener, sneak off to his office and work the speed-dial all period. Who were you calling, Gilles? Your women? Your agent? Bookie?"

"I never needed an agent." He picked and strummed as he spoke. He said to Dave, "*Ça va, monsieur?* Just soaking it up, *non? Tortue au grand soleil.*"

Dave lifted his glass in salute.

In an approximation of a German accent, Rob repeated the name Strudel Haus as he ran his finger down the page.

"Clarisse, can you come find this number for me? I must be going blind."

She got out of the pool where she had been standing with Becky and took the phone book from him. "Ess tee, not ess aitch," she said.

Rob found the number and dialled. He stood up and moved to the far end of the pool. "Sorry," he said, "say again?" He put a finger in one ear and listened with the other. "Who? Lanford? You're making this up."

Gilles was singing "Miss Otis Regrets" the way the Mills Brothers used to do it. As Rob traced the far corner of the pool, pacing, hunched like Miles Davis doing his best to ignore his audience, Dave had a vision of what had caused the delay at the Strudel Haus.

He sees Byron's father stride into the restaurant. The dishes are being cleared and people are getting refills of coffee in anticipation of the speeches and presentations. Nobody is retiring this year, but various teachers are being recognized for their achievements. Manfred Holtz is getting a twenty-year pin. Jerry Salisbury is receiving a national teaching award. Helen MacMillan, one of the secretaries Dave likes to flirt with, is taking maternity leave. People begin moving their chairs so that they can see the head table, stretching their arms out over the backs of adjacent chairs, loosening belts. The Strudel Haus always feeds them well.

Lanford Day is well known to most of them. He has sold property to a few, has never missed a parent-teacher interview, serves on this year's executive of the home and school association. He is a strong, handsome man with an open smile, the type of person who remembers to ask about your children. Five of his six kids graduated from the school. When he visits, he walks down the middle of the main hall as if he still owns the place, still heads the student council. All his life he has defied obstacles, turned his uniqueness against impediment, won honours in the classroom, on the track and in the chambers of commerce. Nothing fazes him. His nerve is legendary.

Dave sees him walk up to the head table and gently take the microphone from Kate Douglas, the principal. She hands it over willingly. Everyone still aches with him. They would much rather listen to him than to Kate, who is a fine administrator but an uninspiring public speaker. Lanford holds the mike down near his chest so that with his deep, sonorous voice they hear the drum of his damaged heart. He introduces himself with genuine humility, and grows in their esteem.

"I did not come here to talk about my son," he begins, and someone calls out that he should, he has every right. They had held a memorial service for Byron in the gymnasium during school hours, but Lanford had not attended. They need this chance to grieve with him. Closure, they call it. In his business he knows about closure. Without it, a whole domino line of families would be in limbo, homeless. They know that he still feels dead inside. "Speak," they urge him. "Tell us about it."

He does. No-one moves until he has finished. Never have they sat so still for so long. He is the only one in the room not crying.

"I feel no anger," he says, sweeping the room with his gaze, "no hatred for any woman or man. Only pity for one who is not here today. If he were here I would walk up and embrace him. I would say, 'I forgive you, brother, for the worm of discrimination eating your petty soul. I forgive you for what you took from my son and from me. There is nothing you could give me that could ever replace him. I wanted only to look into your eyes and tell you that.'"

They do not look at each other as they wipe their faces with tissues and napkins. The desire to celebrate the end of the school year is no longer in them. They climb into their cars and sit there for a moment before turning the ignition key. The only place for them to go now is home.

Rob folded the phone and let the hand holding it drop to his side. He stood shaking his head. "The bastard."

"Rob, what is it?" said Clarisse.

"Nobody's coming. Lanford Day invited them all over to his ranch. They didn't even have the decency to pick up the phone to let us know."

Mindful of his bandage, Dave got out of his chair and eased himself gently into the water. The smell of chlorine was thick. Janine was carrying Becky piggyback through the water, eliciting periodic squeals from the child as she threatened to submerge like a porpoise. Clarisse walked over to the propane barbecue and bent at the waist to read the instructions for lighting it. Gilles passed through the sliding door on his way inside. Rob got onto a floating air mattress and began talking heatedly to someone new. Dave decided that as soon as Rob was finished with the phone, he would use it to call home. He would say either, 'Honey, I'm on my way' or 'Don't wait up.' He was leaning heavily toward the latter.

Hale-Bopp Calling Vienna

The day after Maddy's trip to Emergency, Vienna found me on the second floor in Bound Journals. The first thing she said was, "Why don't you have any elevators in this place?"

We've got elevators. She knows that as well as I do. She just wanted to have something over me before she thanked me for driving Mario to the hospital. She sat on a chair, took off one of her shoes and started rubbing her foot through her nylons.

"Never mind," she said. "I knew these were going to be murder the minute I bought them." The student beside her was watching her intently. The way she was turned in her seat he didn't have to use his imagination much.

"So nice to see you," I said. But I was thinking, 'Where were you last night and why did your husband have to spend three hours in agony trying to get to a phone?'

She said, "I just wanted to say that if it hadn't have been for you and Hub I don't know what I would've done. Poor, poor Maddy."

"You wouldn't have done anything, Vienna. You weren't home. Mario couldn't get hold of you."

"That's right and I feel awful about it. But the important thing is that Mario is going to be all right and they're going to let him come home in a day or two. Which raises a teensy smidge of a problem. See, I booked this whole next week at the spa—I've told you about the one down in Tempe, it's marvellous—I reserved a place a year ago and I simply can't not go now. You understand, don't you, Lina?"

I wasn't really surprised the day we got Maddy's distress call. At 39 he's got the body of a man twice his age, what with all the steroids and antibiotics he had to take when he was a kid. He refuses to exercise, won't change his diet or stop smoking, insists on driving eight-hour round trips every couple of days just to keep tabs on his doughnut shops.

Hub and I got him to Emergency at the General and, I don't know, I suppose you have to be showing the insides of your body or turning purple in order to get looked at inside of six hours nowadays. Even though Maddy couldn't walk, couldn't stand, couldn't sit—lord knows we couldn't carry him, not somebody just this side of 300 pounds—nobody came out to help him. All we could do once we rolled him out the back of the Bronco was watch him crawl on his hands and knees through the sliding doors. Hub kept saying, "Mario, wait for the gurney, man, someone will come out," but nobody was coming and Mad is not the sit-and-wait-politely sort of guy. His hair was still wet with bath water.

Normally he's got his cell phone handy so he can deal with business problems when they come up. Last month one of his suppliers recalled a ton of contaminated deep-fry oil while Maddy was slowed to a crawl on the 401. That kind of thing would've driven me nuts, but he just turned up the air-conditioning, punched in a few numbers, pulled down a couple of favours and by the time he was doing a hundred again he had new cooking oil being delivered to all ten shops. "Maddy's." You've probably stopped at one for coffee.

I don't know where his cell phone was the night we got him to the hospital. Vienna had it, no doubt. Mario had been taking a bath in that deep new marble tub she begged him to buy. He could've kept running the water until the hot ran out or until somebody found him, but who knows how long that was going to be? By the time we got to him he was lying on his side like a wounded manatee, blue and white in splotches, naked and wet on the floor at the top of the stairs, shivering and yelling. He doesn't remember much of that. The upstairs phone was sitting unplugged beside him, the connection snapped off at the wall. I don't know how Hub manhandled him down those stairs and out to the car.

When he was just a little guy, Mario used to get into bed with me when he was scared, you know, of thunderstorms and things like that. I'd let him put his thumb in his mouth and his other hand on one of my breasts, which soothed him. He'd fall asleep, leaving me wide-awake listening to his wheezy breathing. Every couple of minutes he'd cough because he wasn't getting enough air, and if it got bad I'd go get his puffer for him. He spent so much of his childhood in hospitals. If I could give him his life to live again, I'd make him strong, tall, fast, handsome, a wiseacre, and so dumb everybody would die loving him.

But God decided to give him a defective body and brain three sizes too big. You might as well just pickle a kid like that and put him on display in a carnival. Run an electric current through the brine solution and stand around waiting for the miracle to happen: Brain Boy Breathes Under Water. Whiz Kid Walks Again. Step right up, folks, see a certified Wonder of Natural Science.

Back in high school he was always coming home with prizes. One year he was one of the first to spot the comet Kahoutek with just a pair of binoculars. He used to take the bus south as far as it would go out Riverside Drive past the Hunt Club and the city limits, and then walk out to the airport just to get away from the lights. Kahoutek was a bust, as I recall. People were expecting something big— bigger than Halley. I've read that Mark Twain was born in a year that Halley's Comet was visible and died when it boomeranged around again, 76 years later.

People hang so much hope on heavenly visitations like that. Maddy made observations for about a week and then predicted that this Kahoutek was not going to make much of a splash. I couldn't tell you how he knew this, but he wrote out all his calculations and took some pictures, had them enlarged and enhanced, and entered the project in the regional science fair. One of the judges asked him to suggest a possible application for his method of predicting the size of approaching comets and meteors. Maddy said, "That's not my concern, sir. Knowledge is its own reward." Fifteen years old. He took second prize. They gave the top award to some dope who made a potato-powered egg-timer.

He was always doing that, telling people exactly what he thought, never sugaring over the truth like it was one of his cinnamon buns. He never worried about sparing anybody's feelings. On a full science scholarship—tuition, books, lab fees, room and board—and after getting his degree in two and a half years, graduating at the top of his class, he started working toward a master's in physics, only to drop out after just one semester. The professors were all pinheads, he said, and the guy who was going to be his thesis advisor knew even less about quantum mechanics than Mario did. So he turned his back on science. Sometimes I think science is taking its revenge on him.

But you won't find me feeling sorry for him. If he sold all his stores today, to a Tim's, say, or a Dunkin Donuts, he'd walk away with a fortune. It's taken all my willpower not to say to him, "Mad, give yourself a break, that highway is not getting any easier to drive, and you refuse to take the bus or the train. Give yourself some breathing time. Fresh air, long walks. You could take up golf—Hub would teach you, I'm sure he would—and you could curl with us in the winter. Bring Vienna along."

Sure. Can you picture Vienna on the ice, trying her hand at the broom? If she doesn't have a full shopping-bag in each hand she falls right over on her buns of steel, and that's on dry pavement no less. What he should do is take a good hard look at his finances. Where's the cash flowing? he should ask himself, where's the drain it's going down? He's blind as well as crippled.

Hub told me the other day, he said, "Lina, the man doesn't even have a regular accountant. He has this old retired guy from the church doing his books for him."

Vienna draws directly on the business operating account. No household budget, no savings account to be seen. Hub says they should call the tax auditor themselves, get it over with, save themselves the worry and the wait.

All I'm saying is that Maddy had better watch himself, rein in that woman of his, maybe try to figure out what he sees in her. Which isn't fair, I know. Nobody's got the right to criticize another person's marriage. But this is my little brother. If only you could've seen his face in the car on the way to the hospital. Even after the surgeons got him untangled, hours later, he hardly looked human.

The sorting area at the Bremner is always full. Some days I spend a whole morning just making up carts for the second and third floors. Lately it's been exam time and the old exams—their bindings are falling off, they're handled so much—have to be constantly re-shelved. It's the kind of job where you can't worry too much about things being out of place. I can be shelving ARCH to CHEM, 1994, and somebody will take it right out of my hand and over to the photocopier without even a by-your-leave. I'd love to get Hub to take some of these darlings inside with him for a day or so. Just to open their eyes. Let them see the other side of things, show them how lucky they are with their perfect bodies and sparkling teeth and all the money in the world behind them. Have you seen the cars they drive?

Even so, I wish Hub didn't have to work there. I was driving home from the store the other day, before Maddy's accident. Petey was in the back seat with Trevor from the hockey team. They'd just got new in-line skates, and of course they had to put them on in the car, couldn't wait until we got home. Mind you, it kept them occupied for a while. As we were approaching Disneyland, which is what Hub calls where he works, we had to stop for a road block. At least ten police cruisers were parked on both sides. Cops with big flashlights were pulling cars over. I counted four fire trucks in front of the entrance and then more cruisers, one at each corner of the wall under the towers. The TV news was there, an ambulance, people milling all over the grass between the highway and the front gate. All I could think was, Where's Hub? Is he inside or out? Is it a hostage taking? What if he's one of the hostages?

Petey and Trev had their noses pressed to the side window. Petey was admiring the emergency vehicles and the SWAT team setting up in the back of a big yellow rental. "That's where my dad works," he said. It hadn't dawned on either of them that Hub might be in trouble.

I thought about pulling the car out of the line-up and over to the side of the road, parking, maybe getting out, crossing the big ditch and walking up to somebody who could tell me what was going on. All I had to say was that I was the wife of one of the hostages and they'd hand me a phone. Wasn't that the way it worked? In my mind Hub was already dead and I was thinking, How am I supposed to get by without him? Why did he have to get a job installing alarm systems for Corrections?

Because that's what his training is and it's good, steady, decent-paying work. I know.

Still, not knowing anything about what was happening inside, the boys starting to act up, the other two still at the babysitter's waiting to be picked up, I started to cry. I was so scared that I tapped the accelerator and bumped the car ahead of me. The driver didn't get out or even turn around. He must've been just as jumpy as I was.

"Mom, why don't we just go?"

"Why is he in there?" I said. "God, please, take somebody else, not Hub. Take anybody. Take Mario, for crying out loud, the fat slob. I don't mean that. Maybe I do. You know what I mean, Heavenly Father. Do this one thing for us and I'll never...I'll never..."

"Never what, Mom?"

"Never mind."

It turned out to be a minor disturbance. A bunch of inmates set some sofas on fire, and three of them went missing for a while. The guards closed one section of the prison for a few hours. Hub says the overcrowding is so bad it's a wonder riots don't break out more often. These little smashing parties, as he calls them, are like electrical fuses blowing. It turns out he was working in a different block at the time and got outside as soon as the trouble started. He told us all about it when he got home, which wasn't very long after we did, once we'd crawled up to the road block and submitted to a search. He looked at me and asked why I looked so awful. I wasn't worried, was I? He almost got something thrown at his head.

When they opened him up, the doctors found a split-tailed comet of spinal nerves wrapped around one of Mario's discs. They'd never seen anything like it. Imagine a huddle of them ringing the operating table, looking at each other and scratching their stubbly chins through green surgical masks.

I was reading the other day, in one of the new science journals we get over in Periodicals, that thousands of space snowballs hit the atmosphere every day. Some scientists think all the water on earth could've come from comets. The next logical step would be to suggest that all life on earth also came from comets. I liked the idea so much I made a copy. "Is it not comforting to think that the necessary ingredients for life were frozen inside pieces of cosmic ice that entered the atmosphere of our tiny new planet, melted, mated with the clouds, and rained down amino acids on a raw, unconscious world?" I'd say it is.

When he came home from the hospital I bought a copy of the same magazine to read to Mario, because he'd mentioned he wanted to see Hale-Bopp before it disappeared.

"That's one thing this back injury has forced me to do,"

39

he said. "It's made me stop and look."

'You're still not really seeing, though, little brother,' I thought, looking around the little downstairs guest-room where Vienna had stuck him.

"You used to have a star chart," I said. "You had to turn the dial to line it up with the right date. You had all the names and their positions memorized."

"I remember," he said. "We couldn't get a clear night very often back home. It's better out here. You should go outside with the binoculars."

I was trying to get a glimpse of the comet through the window above his bed. "Eastern horizon," I said, "summer sky. Say, mid-July. What would you see?"

"What time of night?"

"I don't know. Ten o'clock."

"Andromeda closest to the horizon. Alpheratz is the bright star. Pegasus to its right. Cygnus above, and Aquila with...what is it now?...with Altair, the double star, brightest."

"How can you remember that after all these years?"

He just grinned.

"Maybe Comet Hale-Bopp and your back are connected," I said. "If it made those cult nuts go and kill themselves, maybe it's got some kind of weird power over all of us. Maybe it made the nerves in your back go all haywire."

"And maybe you've had your nose in the tabloids for too long."

"Don't you think we—as in I'm talking about all life—could've come from somewhere else, Mad? Doesn't it make sense that in all of space we can't be the only ones?"

"There's only one of you, Lina. That I know."

He tried to shift from lying on his side to flat on his back when suddenly it was like he was being squeezed in some kind of giant vice. Everything locked, his arms, his fists, his head three inches off the pillow, his eyes screwed shut. I stood up, but at first I just looked at him. I love him, he's my brother, but this life he's been handed, this body—nobody should have to make their way around inside a container like that.

There wasn't much else I could do except get him his ice pack and his pills. The drugs did their work and he fell asleep.

He was sleeping deeply when I checked him again. I went into the den and called directory assistance and got the number for Vienna's spa. I got connected to the front desk and the woman who answered said that she couldn't wake any guest at this time of night. I told her that this was an emergency. Ms Dietrich's husband had been in a life-threatening accident. He was in critical condition.

A few minutes later I heard Vienna's groggy, "Hello? Lina? What's going on?"

"Nothing. I think you should come home now."

"What's this about an accident? Is Mario all right?"

"No, Mario's not all right. He's in pain. Or hadn't you noticed?"

"You can't yank a person out of bed in the middle of the night."

"Just get your Size-5 ass back home. Your husband needs you."

I didn't expect her to come home, and she didn't. But I had gotten some satisfaction from waking her up, though, hooking that catch of surprise and annoyance in her voice.

There was no going to sleep after that. I called Hub to say goodnight. He grumbled about having to put the boys to bed, and I told him I'd be home first thing in the morning. Then I took a kitchen chair onto the front step. I like it out there where Maddy and Vienna have built. The comet was hanging just above the top of one of the Hodziks' pine trees across the street. The air was so fresh and cold that it felt like I was sucking in part of the tail and then exhaling it with each breath. All night I sat keeping my eye on that trick of light and dust in the night sky, the miraculous trumpet first there, then hidden in cloud, then peekaboo back again. All the ingredients, the seeds of life, were up there.

Who knew what else?

Give the Dull Boy a Chance

Sebastian was thinking that this year he might finally be too old to crash the graduates' bonfire, when he looked up and saw an earthbound angel mincing unsteadily toward her diploma. She began extending her hand too soon. If she should trip, he vowed, he would not abandon her. He would jump up, help her to her feet, and tell her the soothing lie that he had committed the identical pratfall the year he had been sprung from this fine hell hole. If it wasn't that the electric-blue gowns were long enough for a member of the basketball team to trip on, then it was the fault of the microphone cord insufficiently taped to the stage floor. But she performed the miracle of uninterrupted locomotion on alien heels. He tracked her back to her seat in the third row, and brought his gaze again to the stage, where the teaching staff sat arrayed in hoods and gowns, a glum taxidermy of warring hues upon black. Who were half these people? Some of them looked younger than he was. Had he really used up seven years since his own graduation, flinging himself west, briefly, to muck for a high hourly wage and overtime in the oil patch, and returning to run his father's brokerage before winning any of adulthood's big answers?

He wanted to see the old faces. He wanted Coach Rinaldi back up there, dug out of the ground, his orange Duster parked again in the lot at the south entrance to the school, closest to his classroom and farthest from the main office. Let R.R.'s voice ring out again from the front of the classroom, be it English or geography or typing or business law, he taught it all, or from the sidelines of the football field, where he was ineffectual but much loved: in a 35-year career, 158 losses, 17 ties, 15 wins. Ronny Rinaldi, the man who cut Vince Jacobsen the first day of tryouts, counselling the future CFL Hall of Famer, whose number hangs retired at Frank Clair Stadium, "Try badminton, kid. You'll only get hurt out here."

"Bring back Ronny," he said, loud enough to turn the head of the woman sitting in front of him, Mrs. Hargrove the township clerk, who probably wanted to ask him about the repair arrangements regarding her now not-so-recent car accident, the one in which Charlene Smollet had run her off the Snake Island Road with her yellow Bluebird bus. Sebastian could do nothing about it. The case had to go to trial because Charlene was being charged with dangerous driving. Liability had to be determined and assigned. He had read the police report in preparing his own summary for her company, and could imagine the hush in the aftermath, the tin-can bus full of unrestrained children eerily silent, stopped on the shoulder after having pulled out in front of headlong Mrs. Hargrove on her way to Thanksgiving dinner with her son and his family in Smith's Falls. The big-shouldered Caprice veering right onto the gravel to miss the school bus, just, then careening left across both lanes, then right as if yanked by a drunken puppeteer, then just as violently left again and bellying into the shallow ditch, the propitiously soft-bottomed, soggy depression where she stopped, finally, the frame crimped like a bent aluminum chair, and where she waited a full count of ten before breathing, kissing one of her lives goodbye. The insurance companies would wrangle for a spell, grudgingly bear their share of the cost, crank both parties' rates up a few notches, and move on to fresher game. Sebastian was merely the *maître d'* bringing people and firms together, seating them, preparing them for the course to come. Predicting who would eat and who would be eaten was an even bet.

The woman who had been handing out diplomas to the first half of the alphabet handed L to Z off to Dave Semple, a teacher whose class Sebastian had not taken but someone he drank with on Friday afternoons in the curling-club building across the road from the school. Sebastian's brother Peter taught computer science and was the member who opened the upstairs lounge to thirsty, appreciative teachers and to those who had something more than nostalgia to connect them to Clayton Township High School. Dressed better in his suit and tie than many of them now, their sweaters pilled and picked, their open-necked tweeds threadbare at the elbows and smudged with chalk, Sebastian was respectable enough to have outdistanced their memory of him as their student. If not yet their peer, at least he was no longer part of their workload, and watching him grow into a working man helped them feel connected to the world outside their classrooms. He enjoyed the weekly gathering of men and the occasional young woman, fresh out of teacher's college and naïve enough to believe that she was welcome simply because she shared their workaday concerns, or that she could flirt with one or two of them with impunity. Romances here were ignited to the sound of broom swish and rock roar, leading to more than one marriage, and for a stretch the room would revert to the men again, sloppy in their beer, the talk reaching into dim corners of their lives. Sometimes these Friday prayer meetings brought Sebastian unsolicited business, but he was careful; he knew how quickly the door could close on him should he be perceived to be proselytizing for coverage, increased or new, in life, home or auto.

Sebastian was there to present the Rickman Insurance Bursary to the graduating student who best exemplified the qualities of cheerfulness, industriousness, punctuality and perfect attendance, and who planned to study accounting or actuarial science at the post-secondary level. Mrs. Rickman established the award in memory of her husband the year he died, and it was valued at $300, a significant number because it was the amount of money Gerald Rickman had paid in 1962 to rent the house on Jane Street where he established his business, and where it resided to this day.

Three hundred dollars, a scandalously high sum then, covered the rent for a year. Two years later, Rickman put twice that amount down as a payment to buy the house, the remaining $11,400 provided by a mortgage that Sebastian's father resented his entire life, even for the two decades after the debt had been cleared.

It said something about Ailene Rickman's sense of humour that she should have chosen those four qualities as criteria for the awarding of her prize, for Gerald Rickman had possessed none of them. In a good week he was at his desk three days out of five, and for Mrs. Layton, his office manager, and the one or two junior associates he always found to handle the bulk of the work, usually serious, eager young men freshly graduated from university or business college, these were not the happiest days. They prayed he would burrow into his office at the rear of the building, close his door and leave them the hell alone.

When Sebastian and Peter went downstairs to clean up their father's workbench after his funeral, they found nothing to tidy except a fuzzy coat of dust covering the surface. Hanging by hooks on a pegboard were tools that from the look of them had rarely been used, some never. Baby food jars attached by their rust-fused lids to the underside of the shelf above the workbench held nails and screws, washers and nuts, bolts, pins, brackets, picture hooks, windings of wire and balls of twine, none of which they could remember seeing employed in household repairs. Nevertheless, "Don't disturb your father he's downstairs at his project," meant that they had to wait until after supper to approach him with any problem requiring wisdom or delicacy, qualities which, if he had them, he never showed off in their presence. Still, by the time the dishes had been cleared from the table and Father installed, pipe filled and lit, in his armchair, his platitudinous responses to their requests usually came with an air of magnanimity they mistakenly attributed to his having a full stomach.

46

They did make two discoveries that helped them understand their father better. The first, behind the furnace, in an unused cold room that they had not known about, were hundreds of empty liquor bottles, Pernod being the outstanding favourite among them. The second, in an apron pouch designed to hold roofing nails, was a set of ten pamphlets constituting the lessons of a correspondence journalism course from The Dawson Institute in Cleveland, Ohio. Each one was signed, "G.B. Rickman, Johnsville," in fountain-pen ink across the front, and between Lessons 8 and 9 was a yellow piece of printed paper that read, "*Important. This slip should be completed and sent in with your lesson work. Please write clearly. If you have changed your address write "C.A." in the right-hand top corner.*" On the slip was space to fill in the lesson number of the worksheet being submitted, the student's registration number, the number of the next requested lesson and the student's name and address. At the bottom of the sheet it read, "If an article submitted treats a subject that obviously calls for authoritative treatment, please mention here your special qualifications." The brothers assumed that since he had received all the lessons he must have completed the worksheets for each one, but they found no writing returned corrected by instructors at The Dawson Institute, no unsent first drafts, not even a crumpled false start. When they asked their mother about it, she said the writing course was news to her.

"I always knew he was working at something down there. I just never felt it was my place to pry."

Sebastian was thinking about his father's correspondence course as he stood to one side of the stage beside the table covered with diplomas and awards. The Rickman prize came with a paperweight, a wooden wedge with an electronic calculator embedded in it. Their teachers always chose the winners. This year's recipient, a boy named Jonathan Muise, lived in town and walked to school every day with his twin brother, Jamie. They passed by the front door of the brokerage four times a day. An odd pair, unfashionable in straight-legged corduroy trousers that ended high above white socks and brown oxford shoes, dress shirts with the top button done up, sweater vests, heavy backpacks always balanced on both shoulders rather than slung off one in the casual, sloping way the kids carried them. The brothers walked to school and back twice a day, coming home for lunch rather than eating in the bestial cafeteria. They race-walked, one usually a step ahead of the other, never side-by-side and never conversing. They were unathletic looking, with narrow shoulders, wide hips, large rears and short legs: a pair of big-headed pears. And yet they moved quickly, tilted forward as they walked. Had they made their way in this manner all their lives? Had they never wandered off track, on the way to kindergarten, say, dawdling with a stick at the edge of a ditch, engrossed in the fluid dynamics surging there in springtime, the potential for hydraulic diversion full in their brains? The school buses passed them in the morning and at the end of the day, and their classmates called to them out the open windows, "Moose boys! Jon-a-thong! Janey! Hurry home, Mummy's waiting with pie! Watch out, he's gaining on you!"

If it had been up to Sebastian he would not have chosen either of the Muise boys to receive the bursary. He would have picked the prettiest girl in the senior accounting class and changed the award from a paltry $300 toward her tuition to a summer job at Rickman Insurance, $300 a week at least, giving Mrs. Layton a full two—no, three-week vacation. And summer being traditionally a slow season for the business, he and his award recipient would find themselves engaged in long conversations about world events and human nature and, eventually, the mysteries of love. If she had a boyfriend he would subtly illustrate for her the shortcomings of the adolescent male, and if she did not he would tell her just how lucky she was to be young and beautiful and free. The secret, he would counsel her, was to wait as long as she could before surrendering her heart to one man. Men, like fruit, suffered from too early plucking; she must wait until she had found one who had ripened on the branch. Would he be that forward, that obvious with her? Yes, he decided, he would. He had lost too much time already in polite, indirect discourse.

At the reception in the library he saw the girl who so endearingly had made her way, arm outstretched across the stage, and immediately the fictional person in his mind merged with the real. She had around her a protective husk of family: mother, father, grandmother, little sister, a collective picture of relief and self-conscious pride, all wondering when might be the soonest they could leave without hurting anyone's feelings.

"You didn't trip!" said the little sister, and the exclamations and laughter from the others told Sebastian that they had been thinking that very thing. Was that it, then? Was the secret simply to get through each day without landing on your nose? And if you did, what then? Well, he thought cleverly, pretending that this was their first conversation over coffee in the cool of a July morning, this is the reason we have insurance, isn't it? Our business, denigrated as it is, ever lacking in the respect afforded, say, the legal or the medical professions, is there to be a safety net. Didn't she think so? He would tell her how discouraging it was, then, that so many people were moved to defraud insurance companies, the institutions that picked them up off the floor and dusted them off.

The punch was uniformly peach in colour with pieces of ice and kiwi floating in it. Sebastian dipped a cupful and considered adding some of the vodka he had in an airline bottle in his pants pocket. Like most of the men in the room, he had removed his suit jacket and was holding it draped over his arm. He thought about his father, drinking alone, sitting at his workbench in the basement and scratching away on a pad of paper. Where were his completed lessons? Had he paid for the course and completed all the exercises only to destroy his work? What had he written about? He had pencilled asterisks beside some of the suggested topics in Lesson No. 1: "Overcoming Social Awkwardness," "Gold in Your Attic," "The Art of Happiness," and "If I Could Begin Again." The following sentence, Sebastian remembered, was underlined: "Editors have a particular liking for the article that is signed, 'By a Teacher,' 'By a Gardener,' 'By a Private Secretary,' etc." He wondered how the one 'By an Insurance Man' might read. "In this turbulent age, few people possess the insurance coverage they require for peace of mind." One suggested title had been underscored with a double line: "Sometimes success is delayed—Men who have 'made good' after false starts."

As a boy, Sebastian had appreciated secrecy, honouring what he saw as his father's need to keep hidden the big surprise he had for so long been working on, and so had never been tempted to snoop. Peter, older, never at home if he could be out playing ball with his friends, generally stayed out of the basement because he associated it with weekend chores. In the end the "project" stayed hidden. All that remained was a faint, black licorice smell of Pernod, the smell Sebastian most associated with love and lost causes. It was the smell of the smile on his mother's face as she looked behind her at his father on the stairs, his hands pushing on her bottom. "Up we go, Mother, up-see-daisy!" Her shriek of "Gerald!" Their muffled laughter.

After Sebastian graduated from high school, his father tried to convince him to stay and work for the summer at the office. He tried to explain the nature of the business, but was unable to make it seem anything more than drudgery. The boy needed to break away, to work his muscles out of doors, to see a different landscape. It was boom time in Alberta then, he had friends heading out that way. It had to be done or he could never feel content to return. That was something else he could tell his young protégée: even if someone hands it to you written down in a book, you cannot know at eighteen what you will know at 25.

His father's one public passion had been football, and since he felt it was too far to drive into Ottawa to watch the Rough Riders, he came out every fall instead to watch the Clayton Township High School Spartans play their home games. The end zone of the field abutted the Rickman Insurance property, and Gerald had a gate installed in the fence. He liked to sneak out the back door of the office and stand on the sidelines chatting with Coach Rinaldi and the players. For two years Peter played for the team, riding the bench the first season and tearing the cartilage in his knee halfway through the second. Because it got him out of his last class of the day early, Sebastian volunteered to hold one of the yardage markers, and usually once or twice during the game he and his partner on the other end of the chain would have to run onto the field to help decide whether or not the ball carrier had achieved a first down. Seeing his father on the other side of the field made him feel full and agitated, as if he had eaten a big meal and drunk too much coffee. It wasn't an unpleasant sensation. Thinking back on it, he realized that this was the only time his father saw him perform in public. He hadn't played sports or a musical instrument, hadn't taken part in public speaking or Scouts or 4H. He knew that his father's attention was riveted on the game and, for the half season that Peter played defensive halfback, on his eldest son. Nevertheless, Sebastian held the tall metal standard as straight as he could, and moved promptly with the referee ahead to the next line of scrimmage, as if the very outcome of the battle could not be decided without him.

Gerald always slipped back through the fence as soon as the game was over, and Sebastian usually stayed to help pack gear back into the gym storage-room, but at home they would talk about the game. Peter and Gerald would dominate the conversation, arguing about this or that strategy, occasionally letting Sebastian interject. From his vantage point it was a game of inches. He could never understand why a player would choose to run so far laterally, and sometimes in the wrong direction, when his objective was to move the ball ahead. It seemed such a waste of effort. Peter was ardent about blocking; in his eyes nothing in the game mattered more. Their father liked to talk about the game as if it were a story. He would identify the points at which errors were committed, energy and fortune shifting away from one side and toward the other. He delighted in the definitive nature of the outcome. Here there was no negotiation, no compromise between parties. Damages were never shared. No statistics had to be consulted to determine loss or liability. When the final whistle sounded, only one group walked off the field with their heads high.

The play during which Peter hurt his knee, Sebastian was ten yards ahead of scrimmage and had taken his attention off the game for an instant to straighten the chain. The way Peter told it, he had pushed one of the opposing blockers to one side and was tackling the ball carrier high around his shoulders when one of his own players joined in the take-down, hitting Peter low in the legs and from the side. After the play, he lay on his back with his good leg bent, its foot pressing into the turf against the pain. Every so often he raised his head. Coach Rinaldi and Dr. Gleeson, the local GP who volunteered his time as team physician, ran onto the field, and they called for the stretcher. Sebastian watched from one side of the field, his father from the other, as they carried the boy off. Sebastian waited for his father to move. He could hear Peter crying. The doctor gave Peter an injection and packed his knee in ice, and the stretcher bearers carried him over to the ambulance when it backed close to the field a few minutes later. Play resumed soon after, and when Sebastian looked again, his father was gone.

He just assumed that his father had ridden with Peter to the hospital in the ambulance. They played the last quarter of the game, Clayton losing, surprising no-one. People shook their heads and laughed, calling, "Maybe the next one, Coach," to Ronny Rinaldi, who always took it cheerfully. Sebastian was helping stow the yardage marker and the extra footballs in the equipment-room when Coach Rinaldi found him. He said he had just got off the phone with a nurse at the hospital. She needed Peter's health insurance number and a parent or guardian to sign the release form.

When Sebastian got to the office, Mrs. Layton told him that his father had gone home early. His mother greeted him at the door of their house, which was only two streets away.

"Your father came home complaining of a migraine. He lay down for a while and now he's downstairs working on his project."

Sebastian told her about Peter's accident. He didn't tell her that his father had been at the game and had watched Peter being carried off the field.

"Let's not disturb him with this," she said. "It will only upset him."

Peter was being wheeled back into the Emergency Room waiting area when Sebastian and his mother arrived. Doctor Gleeson met them and said that the knee, now strapped secure in a brace, would probably require an operation. He would make the appointment with the surgeon for them. It was the end of the football season for Peter, he was afraid, too early to tell about next year.

Sebastian was about to introduce himself to the angel and

her family when Jonathan Muise appeared at his elbow. Standing behind the boy were his brother, and a man and woman whose physiognomy made the familial connection irrefutable. The man gave Jonathan a gentle prod.

"I just wanted to say," he began, holding the paperweight up in front of him with both hands.

"Hello. Congratulations again," said Sebastian. A title from one of his father's pamphlets flashed in his mind: "Give the Dull Boy a Chance."

"This, um, prize is really...I mean...."

"Barry Muise, hi," said the man, stepping forward to shake his hand. "Policy holder, Gold Key Mutual, home and auto, hahaha! This is Mary Louise, my wife."

"Nice to meet you," said Sebastian. His eye wandered to where the girl had been standing.

"This means so much to Jon, you know. He's not a really outgoing boy, not like Jamie is, and, well, talk about a boost to the old self-esteem. Am I right? Not to mention the pocket book. Tell Mr. Rickman about your plans for it, Jonathan."

Gone. No, there they were, filing out of the room past Dave Semple and Peter, who had appeared in the doorway. The men had doffed their academic robes and were now in jeans and short-sleeved shirts. Dave pointed to his watch and then mimed the action of holding a steering wheel. From the flush on his face, it looked like Semple was a few drinks ahead of everybody.

Jonathan found his tongue. "It's a toss-up between Algonquin College and Sheridan. Mum doesn't want us moving so far away, so she's hoping I'll choose Algonquin. That's where Jamie's going. There's pluses and minuses on both sides."

Maybe she'll show up at the bonfire, he thought. Not likely, from the look of the protective phalanx around her. It didn't have to be her. Someone like her. Someone who might discover him.

54

"I was wondering," said Mr. Muise, "seeing as I got you cornered here—hahaha—if I could ask you a hypothetical question about a claim."

"Sure," he said, holding up five fingers and pointing out the window to the parking-lot. Dave and Peter waved their acknowledgment. The boys and Mrs. Muise moved away a few steps to allow their father to speak to Sebastian, who made an effort to listen, pulling his ear back as his attention wandered away from the speaker. The room had been renovated since his time there as a student, not that he had spent much time working in the library. The worktables were larger, the computer terminals newer, the lighting better. Were there more books than he remembered or were they only displayed more prominently? Current issues of periodicals were arranged on freestanding wooden display cases.

Mr. Muise was telling him about a friend whose heating oil tank had leaked fuel into a neighbour's basement. He laid the details of the case before Sebastian the way a trial lawyer builds an edifice of evidence for a jury. The droning voice faded, and Sebastian's attention returned to the magazines. His father had dreamed—who knows for how long —about writing for the popular press. "If your work is to make strong human appeal," the first pamphlet advised, "you must study patiently and sympathetically what interests the average man and woman."

Since discovering the pamphlets in the basement, Sebastian had wondered what kind of writing his father would have done. He assumed that it would have had something to do with business, that he would write profiles of successful entrepreneurs or articles telling people how to invest their money wisely. He had envisioned a weekly column, "Ask the Insurance Man," guiding readers through the labyrinth of policy options. He watched Mr. Muise's mouth. That wasn't it at all, he realized. We aren't what we do, not unless we are very lucky. He looked out the window

55

to see his brother and Dave Semple and a group of other men leaning against the rear bumper of Dave's car as they sipped from cans of beer in the failing light. Their talk was indistinct to him, their intermittent laughter musical.

He was going to have to say something to extricate himself from Mr. Muise. He was thirsty, craving that first clean mouthful. He felt the draw of the tailgate party, and beyond it the bonfire in whose short-lived light he could be a boy again. *I'm sorry, sir, I haven't been listening to a word. The art of journalism is the art of being interesting. Your "friend" will probably have to let the courts decide this one. You can't be interesting without first being interested. Your son is a dull, dependable boy who will go far. No doubt he takes after his father. We who take after our fathers are the backbone of society, wouldn't you agree? The secret is not simply to follow in his footsteps, but to widen the path. That's what I did, took a floundering business and whipped it into shape. Don't get me wrong, I like what I do. I'm good at it, better than he ever was. Why do I take no delight in it, then, I ask you?*

The kind of writer his father would have been? He thought of Irwin Shaw writing about the Army-Navy rivalry, Haywood Broun revealing the royal heart of Secretariat, Norman Mailer seduced by Muhammad Ali in Kinshasa, Peter Gzowski analyzing Wayne Gretzky's genius for anticipation, Don DeLillo seeing Joe DiMaggio through the eyes of a gate-hopping, worshipping boy. His first published piece? It would have to be a profile of Ronny Rinaldi, the winningest coach in high school football. That, he thought, as he put a hand out to touch Mr. Muise's elbow, gently but firmly in the non-threatening way that said he was sorry to interrupt, but he had to leave now, that would be worth the read.

To Esker Bay for Viking Brides

The Twin Otter makes one rattling pass, circles back out of sight behind the trees, and emerges directly overhead, nosing down into the wind. It bounces twice on the chop before settling. As the plane turns toward him, Leo turns back to his fire. He feels shave-and-a-haircut knuckle-rapped on his helmet.

"Leo! What's the difference between a duck?"

Through the cage of his mask, Leo blinks at the boy who is some mother's son she'd once cradled in her arms and whose yellow curls she'd wound round her fingers. Leo grunts, jabbing with his hockey-stick handle at a piece of gristle that isn't burning properly. He knows this is going to be one of the long nights.

"The difference between a duck is twelve. You need more juice there," and the lad sprints down the corduroy to the water.

"No, leave it there. Beak. I don't need none of that."

The boy returns with a jerry can pulling down his right arm from the shoulder.

"Then you just wait till I'm far enough away."

Leo steps carefully along the log path. He can't make his eyes stay in focus through any single square of the mask. He shuffles a two-step back up toward the tents, his sloping back and shoulders rippling waves of exertion like those of a bear at the retort of a rifle. He can hear the plane complaining as it approaches the shore. Before Leo can plant his feet and turn, the physics major, Mouse McFarlane, yells, "Da blane! Da blane!" and tears out of the cook tent, arms whipping in different directions like rotors.

"Track! Track! Clear the way, O Toothless One!" and he clips Leo in passing, sending the older man sprawling back hard on his tail on a rock. Leo bites his tongue as he lands. He thinks about the plush lawn in front of the Edmonton airport.

The plane presents its length, filling the space between the trees where the path opens onto the rock beach. With the red-and-white fuel drums beside the little dock, it ruins the line of the horizon. Hands under his armpits pull him upright. Maurice, the boss.

"You're a smart one to wear that get-up, Leo." The geologist looks toward the lake. "Expecting anything special this time?"

Leo is expecting a half a kilo of French roast that he will grind by hand and then brew in his own manual drip and carry with him out on the lines each morning in his one-litre steel thermos. Oh. Oh!

He knows that Maurice is expecting the computer he has been asking for for two years. Every camp, he makes the same request. Every camp, a differently worded denial is returned. It is too cold to run it in the winter. It is not securable against theft by "those who will remain unidentified" in the summer. Not safely portable in the fall in New Brunswick. What about a light-table, something, anything to make the job easier? He said the same thing to Leo over scrambled eggs in the Bessborough in Saskatoon that he said over hash browns in the Travel Lodge in Uranium City: they can afford helicopter fuel at thousands a day, but they won't dish out for the mapping technology that could probably sniff out a mine all on its own.

One obstacle is the project geologist, Manfred, he of the safari suit, who materializes once or twice a season to murder hope with his niggling inspections. "One cannot carry out good geology on an electrified box." Once he found a mosquito squashed bloody at 120.25 W. / 327.63 N, and torched the contour map that Leo had been tracing squinty-eyed half the night, right there in the tent. The memory makes Leo shudder.

Leo knows that the musician, Spliff, is expecting grass. He is craving grass. He is going to run naked into the bush after Labrador Tea to smoke, and soon if it doesn't come this time. His playing is beginning to sound stormy, mournful, a bottle broken against the brick wall of his graffiti need. He wants them all to call him Harp. His long black hair, tucked behind his ears, hangs greasily from under his wool skullcap. Ever since the bear, the one they finally had to shoot, ran the wino cook back to civilization on the plane two weeks before, Spliff has made breakfast and supper, a quotidian arrangement he prefers to the monotonous prospecting. During the day he mans the radio or plots data. If the kid ever woke up completely, thinks Leo, he'd be terrifying.

Mouse is expecting love letters and acid. The Beak is expecting porn. All except Leo, who is dry now twelve years, are tasting that first beer. 'On the other side it is dry, / But here it is beer.' Leo is expecting his first Disney stock, not the certificates themselves, which he's had sent to his mother, but proof of purchase. Japan and Europe are poised to embrace Mickey. They are building a floating theme park in Tokyo Bay. 'Apple, 'tendo, Texaco, / These pale lights will come and go, / But Donald Duck and Chip and Dale, / They endure to tell the tale.'

Leo feels the heat blast against the bristles of his cheek. Mouse skids to a stop, all two pear-shaped metres of him thrown back on his heels like one of Walt's goofy creations. The tongue of flame laps up into the poplar leaves above the rust-brown garbage drum. The Beak shrieks. His cap is gone. There is smoke coming off him. He runs onto the dock, from which he belly flops into cold Athabasca.

When he emerges, his black T-shirt hangs like drapery from his shoulders. The plasticized decal, what used to be gory dagger points forming the name of a heavy-metal group, is melted. His eyebrows and lashes and forelock are gone. He stops. No-one moves toward him. Leo thinks, 'In case of shock, have victim lie in prone position on flat, even surface, preferably insulated from cold ground or pavement.

59

Elevate feet. Cover victim with blanket or coat. Place rolled blanket or coat, or pillow if available, under head. Keep victim warm. Administer warm liquids sparingly.'

The burned boy turns a smile loose on them.

"Bee-eh!" he banshees, one fist thrust skyward.

In unison they all reply, tentatively, "Eh!"

"Bee-aye, you scum-suckers!"

"Aye!" in chorus, full-force.

Then he takes hold of the shirt at its hem and yanks it up over his head, leaving an angry red patch on his skinny tummy.

"Boss, you're not sending me home for this."

"Is that a question, Beak?" says Maurice.

"Who didn't mark the chopper fuel?" says the boy, shivering now, his smile flashing on and off with the chattering of his chompers. His face is beginning to swell.

Leo thinks, 'In all cases of trauma, the leading cause of death is not the injury itself but untreated shock.'

"Go and get warm, you jerk-off menace to humanity. Come on," says Spliff when the little guy just stands there. Spliff takes off his Rasta cap and pulls it down over Beak's plastered locks. Then he leads him up the path to their tent.

"Get him into his sleeping-bag. Dry him off first or you'll ruin the down fill, Michael."

Spliff says, "Should I take his pants or his shoes off first, Boss-man? Should I dry his little weenie with a towel? Should I powder his bum-bum?"

"All right, all right, just do it, please."

Leo has worked with "Moe-reece" long enough to know that the geologist is more comfortable alone in the field breaking schist with a rock hammer or running a mag survey than he is being a leader of men. This kind of incident, which happens at least once a camp, usually close to teardown when the crew is beginning to get careless and giddy, not concentrating, horsing around, splinters Maurice's composure. He turns to Leo.

"Look. If you're going to be in charge of the garbage, then be in charge of the garbage. You won't let anyone else near it, at least you never did before. What's going on, Leo? Are you bushed or what? Should I send you home?"

There is no need to say that. Maurice knows what care Leo takes with the job every day after supper, no matter how tough a slog the day has been. If something does not burn, then he makes sure it is covered in soot and sealed in a plastic baggie and buried deep in the rocky ground.

"I don't fight with someone. If someone wants to go do something foolish, then that's his own fool right. Me, I just ask for time to get out the way."

"Okay, I hear you," says the geologist. Then, because it is easier to switch topics than to apologize, he says, "Wonder why the flight's in so late tonight?"

Mouse has the mailbag hoisted above his head. He is enjoying teasing the rest of them who stick their feet into his path and punch him and jump high in vain.

Spliff threatens, "Open that sack, you white Watusi, or I'll make you swallow one of your little drowned victims."

Mouse relents. He stops, places the heavy canvas mailbag at his feet, and unties the cords cinching the opening. He begins to hand letters and packages to those crowded expectantly around. Then he catches himself.

"Oh, sorry, I guess you want to do this, Maurice?"

"Just keep it moving, Mouse. She's sending a super-eight for me to preview. The projector's oiled and ready to play."

"Oiled and ready to play, Maurice?"

"Continue, please. Con-tin-you!"

"Spliff. Spliff again. Spliff encore. Smells like contraband. Leo. Hooters. Feels like smut, Vanderhooten. Anything you want to confess? Varney. Varney, do your people actually read and write? Sasquatch. Lips. Phil Blum, esquire. Whoa, Maurice, a big fat one. I think this is it. I don't see a Censor Board rating stamp on the wrapper. I'm not sure this shouldn't be sent right back unopened. You are so welcome, Bwana. Beak. Is Beak still alive? Monster Truck Annual. Scintillating."

They open their letters where they stand or sit there on the makeshift boardwalk, or shuffle blind, reading, to their tents. Leo enters the tent that he shares with Beak, Spliff and Mouse. The boy is asleep in his Five-Star, only his damp hair visible. Leo slips Monster Truck Annual into the pack that hangs from a wooden upright beside Beak's head. He watches the sleeping-bag rise and fall, rise and fall. If he had fathered a boy at this boy's age, he could be Beak's papa now. If he had bought Mitel at 50¢ a share when he had had the chance, he'd be...where would he be? Still doing this, he reckons. If he had died at 20, had his body frozen as he is going to do when the time comes—the arrangements are in place—and had come back to life now, he would not understand these young guys any more than he does now. Probably less. If, if, if. If he had not taken it upon himself to uphold certain standards of sanitation in the camp, they would all have been eaten by now.

He sits on the foamy of his own bunk below the boy's, and opens the package from his mother. She has written:

Dear Leo,

I hope you are warm and dry and watching your intake of caffeine. You know your limits, Son. I had a difficult time finding these organic beans because The Perky Perk in the Palmetto Mall closed down just after you left. It's sad to see now. Half the spaces are empty. When Selena drove me by there the other day, it looked like somebody smiling with a whole bunch of teeth missing.

I put your stock certificates in the safety deposit box at the bank. I was helped by a very pleasant woman I'd never seen before. She is supposedly an assistant manager, but I have my doubts because she was wearing orange pajama bottoms that you could see her underwear through!

A terrible thing happened to Mr. Zwicker. You remember he's renting downstairs. It was our intention to walk together along the bicycle path all the way into Waring Mills to see the new Robin Williams, but part way there Mr. Zwicker's bladder let him down and he insisted that he hail a taxi to take me home. Well, you know how easy it is to hail a cab out there on the highway unless Selena happens to be driving by. I told Mr. Zwicker this and his response —I think he's quite taken with me—was to step gallantly into the path of an oncoming car, which was in the process of coming to a stop, although not before it took out most of what was left of the old fellow's hip. So, instead of seeing *Popeye*, your poor old mother sat most of the evening in the Emergency Room of the General, waiting to hear if Mr. Zwicker was still alive, which he was, luckily, because he is behind two months on the rent.

Son, I know I say this every letter, but it bears repeating. I think you are getting a bit too old to be traipsing through the wilderness of northern Saskatchewan after uranium, so why not get a good sit-down job here like your nephew Dwayne over at the gravel operation. It's all automated now and extremely safe.

Your loving mother

Leo opens the tabs that close the brown paper bag of beans and dabbles his fingers in. He brings his nose close to the dark, almost black nuggets, puts one in his mouth and chews it between his gums, he is so starved for it. He reseals the lined bag, finds his Pyrex pot, his plastic filter cone and his cloth filter all in their box on the floor under the bunk, and heads up to the cook tent with these treasures in his arms.

The expediter in Eldorado knows by now to include a good coffee grinder with whatever kitchen supplies are being shipped to the camps where Leo works. This is his second summer at Otherside River. He has also worked at Fond du Lac, Stoney Rapids, Esker Bay and Poplar Point, whose grid had been obliterated by a forest fire in the spring. Everywhere he goes, they have heard about Leo. Hava-Java Boucheron. Monsieur Coffee. He should be Flat-Out Jumpy Leo, but he isn't. He is steady, plodding, never-get-angry, do-the-job, dependable Leo.

The puckered beans rattle together into the grinder's cup. He replaces the lid and pushes down as he turns the crank. The aroma released is almost enough. Now he inhales it, the smell unlatching pleasure doors leading directly to his brain. He fills the kettle from a bottle of boiled water he keeps cold in the propane refrigerator. The stove's blue flame licks the kettle's belly.

From outside come the excited sounds of the crew unloading the plane. Cries of "Bee-eh! Bee-aye!" The rule is that none of the beer can be opened until everything is safely stowed. Leo has a case of 24 coming to him for finding the hottest rock of the summer, a zinger that made his scintillometer squeal off-scale as he held it in the air over the boulder. It was not hot enough to X-ray him or shrivel his jewels, but it was important data. "An important find, Leo. We're on our way to a mine here, I can feel it," Maurice bubbled. Leo thinks about the things for which he will barter with his winnings. Bug spray. Chocolate bars. Shaving cream and shampoo.

The geology, as he understands it, works this way: the whole area, the lake and everything on this side, what the Chippewa called Otherside, all the way south to the Shell claim, is glacial and alluvial till, just boulders as far as the chopper can fly, as far down as a worm can wriggle. There is just enough soil to hold a skin of scrub spruce that is so dry it can ignite mid-summer at the slightest spark. Conifers, weed trees near shore, some reindeer moss, but for the most part boulders that had to have come from somewhere originally, carried by ice and water a great distance. The trick is to trace the limits of the gigantic fan of debris, hundreds of thousands of hectares of it, back to a single point where lies, in theory, a mine that will keep the toasters of the world hot for a few more edgy, borrowed years. 'And don't talk to me about plutonium,' thinks Leo. 'I don't know nothing about that bomb foolishness.'

Spliff, white boy with a dark chocolate soul, comes in with boxes of sirloin, which he deposits in the freezer chest. Leo groans as he dampens the grinds of his coffee with the just-boiled water and anticipates the rich acid taste on the back of his tongue. Steak nights are the only time he misses his teeth, which are also in safekeeping with his mother. He'll have eggs instead. He jumps at the dull clang of a full propane tank set down behind the tent. The Otter revs for take-off. Then Mouse is suddenly inside, pushing cooking implements aside, rummaging in drawers.

"Aluminum foil, aluminum foy-ul, al-you-min-ium foil!"

"In with the pots under the stove," says Leo.

"A-ha! That's not enough. We need more. Did any more come in?"

"What do you need with that?" says Spliff.

Mouse leans closer and whispers, "Tonight. It's on. Esker Bay. Scourge of the North." He winks behind his fogged glasses. Then he rumbles out, Kodiaks turning the plywood floor into a kettledrum.

"What's he talking about, Leo?"

"You're asking me?"

"Lawd, lawd. Dis bloke, he be fashion no fine. An' dis blace, she be some wonder-piggery dis after-night. Me," confides Spliff, whose heroes are Sonny Terry and Brownie McGhee and anyone who rejoices and mourns in the same soul key, "I be incognito for dee next hour."

"I read you," says Leo.

"My man!" says Spliff, who slaps Leo's open palm before he leaves him alone in the tent.

Lovingly he fills the cone with water, and when that has drained, he sluices the wet grinds off the sides so that they are bathed again in their own peculiar alluvial muck. The extract, oily, opaque suspension of his one remaining addiction, makes of the clear pot a deep, dark pearl. He lifts it off the burner and looks through it at the summer's inexhaustible light. The hot liquid glows red with promise.

The Beak comes in moon-faced and hungry. He wants to know what has happened to his cap. Leo tells him that it has burned. As he becomes more awake, the boy keeps rubbing his forehead and fingering where the blond down of his puffy cheek used to be.

"You mean it's gone?"

"Beakless Beak."

Harmonica sounds, like a happy train chugging over the crest of a mountain, workmanlike, pneumonic, fill the spaces between the tents. A musical hard-on. On its trail, a pungent, burnt-rope smell wafts down from the far-off crapper. High Harp on top of his world, his two finest pursuits combined.

Mouse materializes in the doorway again. He has wrapped an arm's length of new aluminum foil over his head and under his chin. A half-full bottle of beer dangles, suction-held, from his bottom lip. Leo hears a familiar plop and scrabble from under the floorboards.

Mouse makes his traps from an empty but still-slick lard can, half-filled with water, and a tongue-depressor balanced on the can's lip and held in place with a bit of wire. One end of the teeter-totter rests on something solid at the same height beside the can. The other end reaches out over what is for mousie a deadly well. Lured by cheese placed just out of reach, the animal unwittingly walks the plank.

Every morning at breakfast the student announces casualty numbers.

"Bingo!" says Mouse, catching the bottle. "Now treading water, Bachelor Number Three!"

He croons, "Tonight, tonight, is not like any night..."

Leo feels another shiver that even the glorious coffee cannot fully calm. There are many dangers. He sees his constant job being the preparation and maintenance of defenses: an extra lifejacket in the boat, a flare and water-proofed matches, desiccated rations in a secret pocket sewn into the lining of his poncho, the hockey goalie's helmet and mask, a pocket-sized foil blanket. He takes all these precautions, yet these boys operate outside the bounds of his preparedness. He never knows what they are going to do next.

Beak nibbles a scrap of cheddar. "Bee-air," he muses, his forehead working where there used to be eyebrows.

"Beak, you in for tonight?

"In for quoi?"

"Esker Bay."

"Zee woomans?"

"Yes! Vikings on the warpath! Norsemen of Otherside River. We will raise our sails, approach by sea. Invading, pillaging, wooing, et cetera, et cetera."

"Vikings."

"Are you in?"

"It's an hour, at least, each way, without a wind," but already the tall boy's exuberance is working. Beak begins to smile like a delighted baby. Leo pours and sucks back another cup of hot black. Outside, the mouth-organ dopplers like a flat-out transport first bearing down and then fading on the lonely highway. From the mapping tent comes radio music: Chevalier's "Avery leet-ell breeze seems to whees-pair Louise..." Behind that the sound of the gas generator juicing up a car battery so that the bug-dumb boys can drool over Lonnie Anderson for half an hour, the duration of this particular Die Hard. Then they will trip dreamily to bed. Or will they?

Or might they not forego WKRP's buxom bombshell for a shot at reality: the two twenty-something women running an EM survey out of Esker Bay? Leo knows the answer. He has heard their voices on the two-way just the same as everyone else and, he has to admit, has engaged in a smidge of fantasy himself. But now he is just plain slow, older by decades than most of these isolation-crazy bucks, his responses callused over by thick, hampering scales of habit and loss. He likes being on this cycle that takes him north from May until September, down east from September until freeze-up, home to Clayton for the winter, and back to Athabasca as soon as the ice breaks up enough to allow the float planes to land. He wakes, he takes readings, he eats, he moves along the gridlines laid down by better men, the ones who are paid to make the decisions. He is the one who burns the trash in the evening. He concentrates on remaining unharmed from day to day.

When he looks up, the pot is empty. He can't remember finishing it. While he works the grinder again, he remembers that he is going to have to fly in the helicopter in the morning. Maurice told him about it at supper. They need to take another close look at a section deep in the middle area of the claim before dismantling the camp. That means a whole added layer of anxious mental preparation for Leo. He tries to recall the safety rules about how to get into and out of the death machine, but all he can squeeze out is the feeling of terror of his last flight, piloted by the dead man, the one with the baby-soft hands. He hears the sound of the pudgy man laughing, laughing at Leo's sick face as they hang upside-down before plunging.

First the sky blinded him, then the lake rushed up to drown him. The dead man smelled like Halston cologne. Ridiculous, a man in the bush smelling like that and dressed for nine neat holes of golf before an evening on the town. His fat little fingers worked the joystick, thumb rolling the control ball on top, flinging Leo's stomach all over the cramped glass bubble. "Whatsamatter, Leo?" he heard in the headset, "ain't you never been to Disneyworld? Ain't you never been on one of them twirly-whirls? Well, this here's a whirlybird. Careful you don't hurly-hurl in my whirly-twirl!" The pilot pulled out of the dive to make the aircraft skim the surface of the water like an osprey, bouncing its pontoons playfully. Then they had gone too far past the camp, and were swooping up a rise, just clearing the trees, and then tilting into the open maw of Otherside River, into a serpentine tunnel of trees above the stream that coiled around on itself, the pilot chattering all the while in stereo, something about missions, the Mekong, "offing all them slants."

Another time, at the end of the day, Leo blistered his palms on his axe, two hours clearing a landing space, and the helicopter, when it arrived, hung stationary, alien over the trees, then flew slowly down the gridline, leading him all the way back to where he had begun to take readings. The dead man pointed him finally into a loon-shit bog where he sunk armpit-deep into it, his pack and equipment held dry above his head until he could fling it in the open door. The laughter again. "Sorry I cain't give you a hand up there, pal, but somebody's gotta keep this baby steady! Ally-oop!"

The last time he saw the pilot was the day of the last supply Otter, two weeks before, when the boys replaced their body fluids with beer and went chasing after each other around the tents and knocked over a propane tank, causing Maurice to come out and berate them about what might have happened, his voice cracking under the cold sober reality of it. Leo and the pilot had been right there in the cook tent. Leo was bathing his insides with a brazen Brazilian blend while the flyboy drank lemon schnapps and challenged him to a variety of contests. Leo refused to chug beer, flip coins into the man's mouth or eat a raw onion. He relented to a game in which they competed to see who could click the highest number on a manual counter in two minutes. The pilot won handily, the thumb of his right hand a supple sense organ unto itself. Then he looked at Leo's prickly, sunken jowls and began to laugh that laugh again, a disgusted, half-soused snicker that said he would suck out Leo's very heart and breath if he could, if it meant anything to him to do so.

"Not too soon I'll see the last of your slack arse around here," said Leo bravely.

The pilot answered by planting his elbow on the table, presenting his bare forearm and unfisted hand. "See what you're made of, Swamp Thing."

His smooth, puffball palm was what Leo thought a young girl's breast might feel like. He wrapped his paw around the little hand that had caused him such alarm in the air. The resistance there startled him. It was such a fat and hairless arm. Such a blatant perfume assaulted his nostrils.

The instant the contest began, Leo felt his vitals turn liquid. He gripped the edge of the table with his free hand the way the pilot was doing to give himself leverage, and wrapped a foot around the leg of his chair. He hadn't done this since he was a kid in school taking on all comers, putting down the wrists of all including his teachers. That victory, those sweet successes—he had defined himself by those and by all the contests, the battering, the scrapping, the running, the lifting. In a way, knowing that a certain path is lit while others are obscured by an act, Leo was where he was because of those bouts of quick violence.

The pilot was breathing hard through his nose. His teeth were clamped. The sweat was beaded all about his fat red face. Leo felt his heart squeezing out between his ribs, his stomach expanding in his throat to choke him. He wasn't convinced he was still breathing. Neither fist gained more than a centimetre's arc of advantage at a time. The pilot was trying to get in through Leo's eyes, but he knew that trick, and he made his focus the statue of joined hands. The coffee was roiling about his innards. He steeled his belly as much as it would consent to be tightened. The dandy was beginning to tire, Leo could sense from the way he was pushing and releasing, pulsing and resting. In a minute, Leo figured his endurance would triumph. The tortoise always outlasted the hare. A helicopter had no logical reason to fly. It was just trickery, a piece of metal whimsy sucked into a vacuum of its own making. But a man walking on his own two feet on solid ground, kilometre after rocky kilometre, in rain and in hot sun—this was no trick.

A bell clanged outside, bad gas oozed around them, the evening light dropped, a repeated drum boom blocked all other sounds from Leo's ears. Then, as if from deep water, the sound of seals barking became dogs asking became men squawking alarm became distinct words of accusation, profanity, denial. Leo woke to the danger in his nose and throat. This wasn't his gas. The strength flowed away from his arm into the other man's, and then he was down. The pilot crowed. Maurice heard the gloating and stuck his head in the door. He told the two of them to get the hell away from the tent and fast and don't either of them make a spark, let alone light a match.

Four days later they heard that the pilot had been found dead, in his trailer in La Ronge, of an embolism. For Leo, who still felt the man's soft, incongruous palm locked against his, and heard the weaponry of his laugh, and inhaled his pungent, bug-loving cologne, it made no sense that he should have died in bed instead of being incinerated at the foot of some rock face, still in harness and thumbing his control stick. The man had jousted recklessly with Death, only to slip into its arms like a dreamy, post-coital lover. When he thought about it, Leo felt as disoriented as he had been in the air that terrible time with his head pointed at lake trout and his feet kicking the blue.

The fashion show takes place while he is making his third pot of coffee. The boys try to dress him up, too, but he tucks in his head and bleats his regrets. Each one has a silver helmet, some with traditional bull's horns, others with lewder representations. Each wears a foil-covered breastplate made from the sides of one of the cardboard boxes the supplies have come in. And each one holds a weapon, a mock mace or a sword or a broad-bladed axe. Heavy-lidded Spliff is there, because it is happening. Poor, blistered, inebriated Beak is going, against all of their amateur medical advice. Mouse is expedition captain. Four others, Billy Vardey, Merrylips John, Bob the Yeti and Topofil Blum, are also costumed for the trip. When Leo sees how nuts and excited they are about it, he almost says yes. He almost says, "Make me a helmet, too."

They are rehearsing a war cry when Maurice and Manfred, the project chief, step through the door. Leo has not even heard the helicopter land.

"Interesting use of kitchen resources, Maurice."

"The guys are doing a bit of the Friday let-loose is all. Aren't you, guys? What's all this in honour of? Hmmm?"

Mouse twists the caps off two beer bottles and presents them to the geologists. He whoops, "A raid for Viking brides! To Esker Bay, to Esker Bay, to Esker Bay vee go!"

The others raise the low gorilla chant, "Viking brides, Viking brides, Viking brides."

"Work is scheduled as usual for the morning, I trust, Maurice?" says ice water Manfred. "Taking the boats out after dark such a distance is something I strongly advise against. After all, this is a place of business, gentlemen, and you are engaged in a professional endeavour here. Much rides on your exploratory successes. Every boulder counts."

Maurice musters a defense. "I don't really see the harm in

it, to tell you the truth. These men know what's expected of them. They know they have to be up and in the field by eight."

"Do they, Maurice? Do they, indeed?"

"What if they had a responsible...chaperone, someone to get them back here at a reasonable time?"

"Ya! What if Leo came along? Leo could crack the whip," says Beak.

Manfred turns his scrutiny toward Leo. "Mr. Boucheron. Well. There would certainly be no danger of you falling asleep, now, would there, Leo?"

The laughter turned his way is good-natured and hopeful.

"No...I don't really...no, guys, this sort of thing, it's not for me..."

A chant of "Leo, Leo, Leo..." is raised. They crowd around his chair and boost him into the air. "Please, Pops? Come on, Leo. Just this once?"

"Even if Mr. Boucheron agrees," says Manfred, "I still strongly recommend against this escapade. You'd be unwise to allow it, Maurice."

Leo grips the sides of the chair to keep from sliding off. He rises and falls in their swell.

"All right! Listen up!" says Maurice. "Quiet! I'll agree to this on one condition and one condition only."

"A minute ago you were ready to let us go unconditionally, Boss," says Spliff.

"This is the way it's going to be. You can do this if and only if Leo agrees to act as leader. What he says goes. Anyone not turned out for a full-day's work by eight tomorrow morning will be docked two days' pay."

"Two days? That's not fair," says Mouse.

"Take it or leave it."

"We can make it," says Beak. "If we leave now, that gives us plenty of time. We can do this. The wind's not bad tonight."

"Vikings on the warpath! Esker Bay! Vikings on the

warpath! Esker Bay!"

"Hold it! Hold it! Leo hasn't even agreed, yet," says Maurice.

"Put me down off this thing." He feels all of them waiting for him, Manfred waiting for him to decline, the boys depending on him, Maurice waiting for him to say something to make the very thought of the lark disappear. He looks around the room at the wildness in their drunken faces, the crude costumes, the close, boozy air. They are all beginning to spin around him. He puts his head between his knees until it stops.

"No. I don't want none of this. I'm sorry. This is not for me. I can't do it."

No-one speaks. He stands. Their disappointed faces block his way to the door.

"That puts paid to that, then," says Manfred. "I would suggest you make an early night of it, gentlemen."

"That's all right, Leo," says Spliff. "Don't worry about it, guy. It was a lame idea in the first place."

They file out, some whispering conspiratorially. Leo empties the most recent cone of grounds into the garbage, replaces the plastic can's lid securely, and rinses out the pot, the filter and his Pluto-the-dog mug. His mouth and tongue feel like an ash tip. He stumbles in the twilight to the privy, empties his bladder and then puts himself to bed.

Beak is beside him, shaking him awake. The tent seems to be full of smoke. Leo is sitting on the edge of his bunk. He looks at the spray can in his hand.

"Leo, what are you doing? Wake up. You're gonna suffocate us all."

"Bugs," he says. He feels his skin crawling with them again. "Gotta get them offa me." He resumes spraying Raid into the air above his head.

Spliff and Mouse are awake now, blinking at him through the haze. Leo can't stand it. The dream has not ended. He is the dead pilot, except that it isn't an exploding blood vessel in his brain that has killed him but insects hatching in his head and crawling all over his body under his skin. He pulls his undershirt off over his head. He sees that his arms and belly are a roadmap of scratch marks. He removes his shorts and stands before them naked, trembling.

"Bugs. Everywhere." He rakes his fingernails through his pubic hair and over as much of his back as he can reach.

"Leo," says Mouse, "get a grip, big guy. There's no bugs. It's just a dream."

"Some dream. I'm still in it. " He begins spraying the insect killer directly onto his skin. Now it is excruciating, a raw stinging joining the sensation of crawling flesh. He will die of it. He is being devoured alive. Coughing, he stumbles out of the tent and runs for the shore. He hears the boys following, calling after him to stop. This is what it is to go mad. This is his own hell. He runs into the water, not stopping until he loses his footing and tumbles ungracefully down into it. So cold, it burns, stops his heart. He breathes water and begins to choke and inhales even more. He lifts his head out, gasping, gagging, unable to stand on the slime-coated boulders.

The boys get to him in time and pull him out and get the water out of his lungs. He lies panting on his side on the dock, covered in his sleeping-bag that Spliff has run back to get. Periodically he retches a dark mixture of lake water and bile and coffee. Each time, the boys clean him off, keeping him warm until he is able to sit up on his own.

The Beak puts a warm beer in his hands.

"No, no. I couldn't drink it."

"We almost lost you, there, Pop," says Mouse.

He doesn't feel the bugs on him now.

The three pairs of arms help him to his feet. With the unzipped bag around him, and the boys attending him, and most of what had been inside him now out, he has a sensation of having been purified. He doesn't feel the least like sleeping. The bush smells new to him, a concoction of intelligent fragrances. His tightened skin tingles but no longer crawls. Every rustle in the undergrowth has a distinct snap to his ear. This is what it feels like. He never knew. He had no idea.

"I don't want to go back to bed."

"Come on, Bugs," says Mouse, "you've had a big scare. Tomorrow comes early."

"What time is it?"

"Eleven-thirty," says Beak.

"I want you to make me a helmet," says Leo.

He sits in the bow where he feels every jolt the aluminum hull makes as it slams down on the waves. Of the two, his boat is in the lead, and he is the first to see each new sight on the big lake. Although he holds the electric lamp, and should be looking for deadheads, he looks off beyond the northern shore to where a string of fire that has been huffing and smouldering all summer glows like a necklace. He reaches up to feel the horns on his head. Behind him sit Beak and Spliff, who pass a lit joint between them and giggle. Mouse, his glasses streaming with spray, sits in the stern with his hand on the tiller, a maniacal grin aimed above their heads. He keeps them in the middle of the channel.

Leo is pretty sure he knows what will happen. When they get to Esker Bay, they will have to cut the engines quite far out and row laboriously the rest of the way in, because the approach is shallow. They will probably have to wake everyone and revive the party. The initial novelty of their costumes will quickly wear thin. The women, if they are like others Leo has met working in the bush, will be as receptive as porcupines. The men of Esker Bay camp will sniff around the newcomers warily. There will be no beer left. In the morning they will have to bear Manfred's self-

76

righteous censure.

Nevertheless, he senses that the wind that rushes by his ears could just as easily be flowing through his body. The bow spray bathes his warrior head, cleansing him. Nothing escapes his hawk eye. Instead of the chill, he feels a spreading warmth. He is still afraid. But now, for the first time since he can't remember when, he is awake.

Mrs. Royalty

Now Myrna had been the Mrs. Judge Roy all her married life, some 43 years, and so, recently widowed and remarried to Horace Aulty (yes, the very same of Aulty Cheese), she might well be excused the fact that she was one of the last to catch the significance of her new compound name. While most still called her Mrs. Roy or Myrna to her face, behind her back, and long before she had even begun reeling in the sweet line of love on Mr. Aulty, they had been calling her 'Her Majesty.'

If you believe legend, Horace Aulty, the closest thing to celebrity in Clayton Township, began to build his fortune with a single cow. The beast may well have been named Bessie. Add what paraphernalia you will: three-legged stool, pungent barn, autumnally lidded pre-dawn sky, the sound of a stream of warm liquid hitting the bottom of a galvanized steel bucket. Should you be determined enough to engage him in conversation after church, near the coat rack with the other men standing in wait for their wives, you will find Horace Aulty to be a resolute and honest man. A quiet, taciturn prize. A man made all the more mysterious for his 70 years of vigorous bachelorhood. A man Myrna assumed was as unlike her dear departed Solomon as is the curd from the whey. A man who kept it a secret, if ever he had loved another woman.

Myrna made certain demands that appeared to preclude her unwrapping her prize all the way. The first was that she refused to comply with Horace's wish that she sell her house, although the building was half the size and twice as drafty as the Aulty place. She was not going to move from the home she and the Judge had built themselves, a miniature castle constructed of the same stone as had been used in both the Ottawa Parliament Buildings and the San Francisco Legislature. That, she proclaimed, was that.

Compliant Horace turned over the maintenance of his farm to his brother's daughter Bethany and her husband, newly-weds themselves and only too thrilled to be moving into the Big House.

The second rift in the alliance came when Myrna suggested that her youngest, Chester, who was back after three years out west, also be allowed to take up residence in the Big House. Young Chet was 30 and between positions, as he put it, a state of being that had lasted longer than either of his marriages. "Between positions" was always paired with the qualifier, "on the verge of a breakthrough," the exact meaning of which depended on the particular venture of the moment. In the last such scheme that anyone could recall, Chet had been awarded a provincial grant to help him construct and sell indoor worm composters. Sales proceeded winningly until he began receiving phone calls from angry people demanding refunds. The vermiculture sets worked remarkably well for about a week and then stopped, the halt coinciding in each case with a sudden infestation of houseflies.

"Look," he said to his lawyer as they reviewed the claims against him, "you go out and try finding a goddam brandling worm."

In theory the Aulty estate was large enough to accommodate a dozen Chester Roys without the risk of their colliding with each other. Horace had built the mansion fully expecting that it would one day house a wife and a brood of children, but as he grew richer and as single women and the mothers of single women grew bolder in their pursuit of him as an object of matrimony, he retreated, hermit-like, into his work. His niece knew better than to object to the arrival of her and her husband's house guest, someone she remembered vaguely to have been a banal clown in high school. She had no grounds for complaint. This was a fine place to live, and rent-free at that.

In his new home, the dark little castle with its narrow hallways and low ceilings, Horace tried not to feel claustrophobic. Memorabilia of the Judge smothered the stone walls: musty hunting trophies, awards from the legal community, framed honorary degrees and primitive art that Horace suspected old Roy had manufactured downstairs in his dungeon of a workshop. Myrna would not let Horace smoke his cigarettes inside, although the Judge's pipes were still prominent in their holder on the mantel, and so he took regular furloughs with the toy poodle, Annette. His work was no longer the refuge it used to be; since passing the day-to-day management of the business over to his younger associates, Horace had very little to do at the dairy except get in the way. His sense of entrapment complete and unbearable, he began taking the dog for longer and longer walks through town, and when that was not enough, he began driving with Annette all the way out to the Big House where he would spend first the mornings and then the entire day until suppertime. The day he called to tell Myrna he would not be home for supper, she immediately called her old friend, Mrs. Palmer.

"Why don't you get on out there and see what he's up to, dear, if it's killing you so much to know?" said Mrs. Palmer.

"Oh, I can't chase him down. He has to want to be with me."

"Perhaps he's taking the time to get to know your son. He certainly has some catching up to do there, wouldn't you say, Myrna?"

"Horace has known Chester since he was a baby, ever since they used to pass him around from hand to hand downstairs in the church hall during coffee time. He was such an active child. I would lose track of him and feel a sudden stab of panic in my chest." She was feeling the same pain now.

"It's another thing for a man to come to know a grown

son, another thing altogether, Myrna. I stand on my own experience of Bill and the boys, and that has been one thorny path, let me tell you. It wasn't until they came to be men that the trouble started. But let's not get into that."

"No, Horace is not the type to seek out another man to find out what's in his heart. I'm trying to think of him, now, the man we have known all these years—I wish I had thought about him as hard as this before I decided to go after him. This all has something to do with me, I daresay, and I'm panicked about it. I really am at a hard loss over it."

"You and Horace have been married scarce a month now. At least you have your time with the Judge to fall back on, but Horace is new to all this. He has to have time to adjust. You can't take a 70-year-old bachelor boy and turn him into a husband over night."

"Judge Roy loved coming home. He really loved the home I kept for him," and she began to weep into the receiver.

"He did. He did at that. Everyone knows how much he did. You go ahead and let it out," said Mrs. Palmer.

As Myrna was drying her eyes, Horace sat contentedly at his old kitchen table. Bethany was adding a panful of cooked ground beef and onion to the pot of chili, the aroma of which swirled around him and bound him seductively to his chair. He took a sip of ginger beer from the bottle and watched his niece's young husband, Gatien, whom she called Gates, gambol just outside the kitchen window with the delighted poodle. Gates was playing the way Myrna was always after Horace to run the dog, but Horace drew the line at cavorting.

Then Chester came in talking on a cordless telephone. Horace watched him open the refrigerator and then just stand there without taking out anything.

"I know what I'm doing," said Myrna's boy.

"Another can of worms, Chester?" said Bethany as she

laid a placemat and cutlery in front of her uncle. Horace chuckled as he picked up his beer and leaned back to give Bethany room.

Chet pocketed his cellular and turned around without closing the refrigerator. "Oh, hello, New Dad. I didn't notice you there. How goes the cheese game these days?"

Horace nodded gravely and took another mouthful from the bottle.

"The Head Cheese. Man of few words. King of all he surveys. By the way, have I thanked you for the room and board? You are one generous padre. Isn't he generous? We is some lucky, we young'uns."

Bethany closed the fridge door and then returned to the stove to stir the chili. Chet continued to chatter.

"This could not have worked out better. To have returned to the hive and the Queen Bee—I mean can you imagine me back in the Tower with Her Majesty? Stifling is not the word. At least when His Honour was still around it gave her someone to fuss over. Don't take this the wrong way, Horace, but you don't strike me as the type who lets people make a fuss over him. So that would leave me with no-one running interference. She'd be back rooting through my laundry again."

Horace finished his ginger beer, pushed back from the table and stepped outside. He could feel something forming in the back of his head, a buzz surrounding a gradually congealing notion. The grey sky was just the blank shade required to set aflame the big maple in front of the house. The dog lay stretched out on her tummy on the grass, snuffling her snout under a heap of leaves that were dry and ready to fly. Horace raised his open hand in greeting. Gates waved back.

"Rain coming. Maybe tonight, feels like," said Gates.

"Not until morning," said Horace.

"Ah," said the young man, knowing there was little else to be said about the weather after such a pronouncement.

He waited uneasily in the pause between them.

"Now, those gutters need to be cleaned out before snow."

"Yes sir."

"Got time, scrape down the peeling spots just under the eaves there. Should be some primer in the basement."

"Will do," said Gates, who had the feeling that preparing the house for winter was not what was foremost on the older man's mind. "You want us to go ahead and match the colour there? Beth's got a fair eye when it comes to that sort of thing."

"Well, all right."

"We'd probably need two litres."

"Go ahead and buy the paint, then. Charge it to the dairy."

"I can borrow an extension ladder from work," said Gates, intrigued now and intent on keeping the ball in play.

"Might just do her myself."

"Really? I don't mind. It's the least I can do."

"Nope," said Horace, abruptly ending the volley.

Back in the kitchen, Horace looked at the table set with bowls of steaming chili and a basket of freshly baked rolls and plates of his dairy's butter, and felt the spinning mass in his mind coalesce to a denser, cooler certainty.

"One thing," he began.

"Yes, Uncle?" said Bethany.

"How many children you plan to have?"

"Children? I don't know. We haven't really talked seriously about it. Gates keeps talking about how he wants a big family."

"Lots of kids, then."

"Well, yes, I think so, if we can afford to."

Horace found Chester upstairs in his room, his booted feet propped on the bed.

"Supper ready yet, Dad?"

"Pack your stuff," said Horace. "Meet me outside in the

car in ten minutes."

"Ten minutes! What's the problem? I didn't do anything, I swear."

"Nine minutes."

He drove Annette and Chet back to the castle stoop where he deposited them. When Myrna came outside to see what was going on, he told her to get into the car.

She turned to her son and said, "Chester, tell me what this is all about."

"I have no idea, Mother."

Horace said, "Just climb on in here, Myrna. I have something to say that touches on the two of us."

They drove east on Number Two through Crane's Mills and then turned north on the Baseline Road.

"Myrna, the first day I saw you I was sitting in church," he said, taking one hand off the steering-wheel. "It was a spring day in May and you wore a spiffy little purple hat that I couldn't keep my eyes off of. Missed most of the service looking over at you. Can't tell you what the preacher said in his sermon. Can tell you that a sunbeam came in through the stained glass right under Our Saviour's armpit and lit up that hat and your pretty face under it.

"I spent the better part of the summer waiting for my chance to win you. You know as well as I do I had plenty of chances. It wasn't a big town back then. Still isn't. Bet you don't remember the Harvest Dance."

"Vaguely," she said.

"You weren't much interested in the boy you were with. I had come stag with my brother. Most the night I stood against the wall, watching you twirl around with every boy who asked you. Then, last dance, Ladies' Choice, you walked right across the room and picked me. I near as died I was so nervous. I can still remember the way your hair smelled of lemon juice. I wasn't much of a dancer, but you didn't stop smiling and listening to me the whole time. You even told me you thought I was swell."

84

"Did I? Well."

"I was all set to ask you out to the next dance, when Davey Roy come home from the war and you married him and I went to work making something out of the broken-down farm I was left with when my father died. I hated that place for the longest time. Caved-in barns and rotten silos. And hated it, Myrna, every time I saw you with him. After a while the bad feeling in my chest got smaller and I just went on working. Every time I found I had money in the bank I threw it back into the dairy, because I was afraid I'd take it out and spend it on a diamond necklace or a sable coat to steal you away with. A person can work to avoid and work to forget just the same way he can use drink to achieve the same ends."

"All this time," she said. "Why didn't you tell me?"

"Wouldn't have changed anything." He glanced at her out of the corner of his eye. "Would it?"

"No, probably it wouldn't have, Horace. But I'm glad you're telling me now," she said, sitting taller in the passenger seat and smoothing out the lap of her skirt. "This makes me feel quite...I can't say, exactly. Girlish, I think." She gazed at his profile, and when he glanced over, she was smiling at him, her eyes brimming and fluttery. "I would have to say I approve, sir."

"That's neither here nor there. Thing is, I brought Chester back with me because I don't have room for him."

"Of course there's room for him."

"There's no room for him if you and I move into the Big House together."

"We've been over this before."

"Myrna, let the boy have the castle. Let him bang around in there. It's sturdy enough, he can't do too much damage, unless he tries to burn the place down."

"Give him some credit, Horace."

"Credit is the last thing that young fellow needs."

"Why are you attacking my son all of a sudden?"

"I'm not. I'm just saying that he needs room of his own and we need to make ourselves part of something bigger."

"I don't understand. Everything was working so well between us."

"For you, Myrna. For you. Not for me. See, there's one thing I want now even more than to turn the clock back 50 years, and that's to be part of a family. Babies, puppies and kittens, hockey practice, ballet lessons, mumps, measles. The whole kit-'n-caboodle!"

He slowed the car and pulled off the road into the entrance to a fenced compound. A series of low, connected green-and-yellow buildings stretched for 200 metres parallel to the road.

"You ever been inside there?" he asked.

"Why, no. Of course not." Myrna wrinkled her nose at the smell coming from the nearby heaps of compost.

"I was working here when I met you. It's cool and dark in there. You have to wear a miner's helmet with a lantern on it. You go in and it's like stepping into a damp bank vault. Instead of gold bars, there are racks and racks, ceiling to floor, aisle after narrow aisle, of white mushrooms. It doesn't smell the way you'd think it would, either. It's like you've pressed your nose down into the leaves on the forest floor. And in each rack are hundreds of tiny white helmets pushing through the soil, and not a single one of them has anything to do with the sun."

"Horace, I fail to see—"

"Come inside with me. I want to show you."

"No thank you. I will take your word for it. Right now, if you don't mind, I would like you to take me home."

"Home."

"Yes. Home. My home."

"That dance, the Harvest Dance when you picked me, do you remember what we talked about?"

"No, I don't. How am I supposed to remember what I said to a boy with whom I danced one dance a half-century ago? Really."

"I told you that night about my various duties here. I told you about how I started off hauling and dumping the old soil. Gardeners would come and buy it by the truckload. I was in charge of that. Then I worked my way up until I was in charge of one whole stage of production. It was a big responsibility. It took the entire song to tell you about it."

"Back when you were a chatterbox."

"You said, 'Will you take me there to see it sometime?' and I promised you I would."

"I don't think I would have said that."

"You as sure as did."

"I don't remember. I'm sorry. Oh, Horace, to you this is a place full of important memories, but to me—I'm very sorry—to me these are just a bunch of ugly buildings full of fungus."

He took hold of the steering-wheel at ten and two o'clock and stretched his arms out straight so that his spine was pushed back into the seat. Then he released his grip.

"Myrna, you've always been my queen. I could take a quarter out of my pocket and look at Elizabeth Two and I would always see you. Every couple of decades the image would change to show your maturity, but it was always you. Sometimes it was a sharp picture, sometimes blurry, depending on the coin. Always the same, though." Then he said in gentler voice, "Come with me, now."

"Horace."

"Come jump with me into another picture, while there's still time."

She turned her face away from him toward the mushroom factory. He knew that she had as much interest in it as she had in the stubble of corn stalks remaining in the field on the other side of the road. Or in cheese. Or coins. Or babies. She had removed herself from him so easily, he wondered what had brought her to him in the first place.

He could well imagine. He was usually right about such things. He was the richest man in Clayton Township because he had nurtured an icy right sense about just such things. Things that had nothing to do with dance cards or sunbeams in church or anything as fragile and dependent upon decay as a mushroom.

He said, "I'll only be a few minutes. I want to bring some fresh mushrooms home to Bethany and Gates. Got my heart set on sirloin for tomorrow. Golly, listen to me. Must be my stomach doing the talking now. I won't be long, Myrna."

She murmured something indistinct.

"Then I'll drive you straight home."

She raised her hand in an abbreviated, backhanded wave, but kept her face turned away from him as she continued to look out the window.

Early Easter

In spring, when brief insults of snow make two-tone corduroy of the farmers' fields, after warm gushing days of promise, little towns like Clayton begin to move and breathe with an urgency awakened by the return of the geese. The same cars leave in the morning and return in the evening, bringing their drivers home from work in the city, but now there seem to be more of them on Main Street, more half-tons parked in front of the Co-op, more young women marshalling children and grocery carts out of Brundidge's, more students from the high school deciding to relive the recent glory of March Break, just the last two periods of a Wednesday afternoon, say, Mr. Morris' science class. "He won't even notice we're gone," they assure each other, building a giddy solidarity.

Sandra Kinnian was pulling out of the supermarket parking-lot when a car passed her on the way in and she saw her daughter, Faun sitting in the front seat. A boy was driving, Sandra couldn't tell if it was Ted or not, she really didn't want to know. Quarter to two in the afternoon on a school day and it felt like someone had removed a baffle from between her and the noisy world. A worker with a sledge-hammer was breaking up a slab of sidewalk that had buckled two years ago in the summer heat. Electric organ music was coming out of Bethel Reformed, or was it the hairdresser's below? She couldn't tell. The bass thump of a car stereo, everywhere the identical rhythm regardless of the song, turned out to be her heart, a liquid percussion filling her ears and surprising her as she sat at the stop sign trying to decide if she should turn around or continue with her itinerary. When she checked the mirror again there were four cars waiting behind her.

She made the right turn onto Main Street, and drove to the end of town, taking the turn north and continuing for fifteen minutes, over the river at the Sword and Garter, and into Waring Mills. She parked in front of the travel agency at the mews and walked in. The woman who usually booked Sandra's flights was not there, and so she was directed to Lorraine. A ginger-coloured spaniel came and sat beside her chair. The dog looked threadbare and saggy.

"That's Christian, our official greeter," said the agent, whose oval-shaped non-glare glasses gave her thin face a Eurasian look in striking contrast to her hair, a shade lighter than the dog's and gathered at the back by a black fabric bow. Sandra had left the house without washing her hair or applying makeup, and she felt that if Vince were to walk in at that moment he would probably sit in the seat next to her, lock his eyes onto sultry and intellectual-looking Lorraine, and not even turn his head to acknowledge the woman he was married to.

"Let me just open another menu. No, I didn't think so. The best I can do for that date is Sonata Tours out of Terminal 3, three seats together, arriving 20:35. There's a direct bus to the airport from Hamilton."

Sandra explained that she needed to book one of the tickets a week ahead of the others. Her sister was coming, staying a week, leaving, and then her mother and brother were coming.

"I'm sorry, I misunderstood. Well, that's no problem at all."

Why did people say, "No problem," when in fact there was? Why were such inconsequential things as wet newspapers, specks in the flour, clashing colours and smelly old dogs that sat at her feet looking bored while waiting to be petted, why were annoyances that used to make her laugh now the stuff of gritted teeth and elevated blood pressure?

"I have two seats together on Canada 3000, arriving March—"

"Wait. I've changed my mind."

"I thought you wanted—"

"I'll take the one you said before, the musical thing."

"But—"

"Three seats together. Perfect. Book it. You take this?"

The woman took the credit card and did a you're-the-boss flip of her head as she turned back to her computer screen. As Sandra watched her type in the information, an electric shiver raised the skin along her spine, beginning at the base, where she was apt to suffer pain if she kept a secret or a complaint to herself for more than a day, and rippling upward in a wave, a little prairie dog working its way north.

When she got home she opened the front door and looked in. Strewn the length of the hallway were clothes, a wet bath towel, many toppled pairs of shoes, a bulging lunch bag, notebooks, pens and magazines. She closed the door and sat on the step, grasped her knees and leaned back. The sun shone fully upon her; once the leaves returned, this would be a darkly shaded spot. She decided to wait ten minutes, and if Aubrey's school bus hadn't arrived by then she would carry the groceries in from the car.

The bus passed without stopping. Some time later the phone rang and she let the answering machine take it. It began to cloud over, and the cold seeped into the backs of her legs.

Ted's car appeared at the entrance to the long driveway and made an abrupt, jerking halt. The passenger door opened. Faun began to get out, but the car started to move ahead again and she was pulled, either by the boy or the momentum of the vehicle, back into her seat. The door swung shut and they rolled to a stop behind Sandra's car. Ted got out, opened Faun's door, and walked her up the steps, his guiding hand at the small of her back.

"Such a gentleman."

"Teddy didn't want me getting my shoes muddy, Mom. Come on."

"My mistake."

"Why are you sitting out here? Aren't you cold?"

"I'm waiting for your brother."

"He has band practice today. Remember?"

Ted followed Faun inside. He was going to show her a new chat-room he had found. Sandra decided she would wait until he went home before confronting Faun with the bald fact of her truancy. Her daughter looked so happy, complete in the costume of love and yet undisguised by it. Just their presence in the house cleared a path for her. She carried the grocery bags in, content to do it herself. She decided that if Faun invited Ted for supper, Sandra would try her best to like him.

The first time Sandra brought Vince home to meet Bibiana and Hugh, her mother asked if he was feeling all right. He assured her that he felt fine.

"A touch of irregularity, perhaps."

"No ma'am, not that I know of."

In the kitchen Sandra asked her mother why she couldn't carry on a conversation like a normal person.

"He looks constipated."

"He's not. That's his look."

"If he were a sleeping bat he'd look happier."

"Oh now you're just being mean."

"Hanging from the ceiling, I mean. Turn that frown upside down. You know, the old ditty."

"This is the man I love. I love his face. We will never set foot in this house again."

As they emerged with cake and coffee, they saw that Hugh had gone to his room and come back with a lump of red plasticine. He had his mother's silver tea service tray at his place, and on it was arranging coin-size doughnuts in three rows of four.

"I always start at one and go that way so I remember."

"One is where? Here?" Vince reached across and pointed to the doughnut in the top left corner from Hugh's point of view.

Hugh closed his eyes and giggled. Sniffing with agitation, he aimed his smile at the ceiling.

"No, silly! Mrs. Patterson would kill you. You wouldn't get anywhere near the deep fryer with that attitude, mister. Oh, corn pipes!"

This is it, she thought, this is the moment. The next 30 seconds will tell. I might as well get his jacket for him right now.

Vince's reaction was to set the lines of his tight-lipped smile deeper, to allow delight—for it was that, without a hint of knotted self-consciousness—to shine from his eyes, and to emit the low, growly chuckle that she replayed that night while she waited for the onset of sleep. He leaned into Hugh's imitation of an adult correcting a subordinate's thoughtlessness, absorbed it the way a retriever will tolerate repeated correction during its training, eagerly, lovingly, with an intuitive eye on the outcome. Who was this boy, she wondered, barely twenty, who failed to be repulsed by her bullet-headed, goggle-eyed, hydrant-shaped brother?

Vince had strong hands with long tapering fingers and almost no webbing between them. He joked, when she took hold of them admiringly in her lap, that he had learned his scales fingering the fleshy teats of his father's cows, his cheek pressed against the oven-warm flanks. She watched him reach gently across the table and coax Hugh—face still tilted up, air pumping in and out of his puny lungs, arms barely able to cross his torso—to show him where the order of operations began and what happened next and what precautions, if any, had to be taken.

Aubrey dropped his French horn and his book bag just inside the door. Sandra hadn't the will to force him to remove his belongings to his room. He was another heat-seeking, mother-dependent presence. He was welcome and she was his Sherpa. Yes, she thought, as he stood before the open refrigerator, it's full.

His father arrived only a few minutes later, and she thought, Now I can breathe. Now the house is no longer an adversary, now I can consider the approaching observance, religious and secular, of the unfurling springtime. She considered what mayhem she had invited by putting her mother, brother and sister on the same flight.

Ted went home before supper. Faun pushed bits of tofu and stir-fried vegetables with a chopstick around her plate until the phone trilled, and she leapt to it as if it were a baby choking. She wandered to the front entrance, halfway up the stairs, down again, into the living-room, the dining-room, the bright reading-room. When she returned to the kitchen table she ate everything left on her plate. She declared that Ted was sweet and attentive, that his mother was whacked because she was angry at him for keeping her car all afternoon when she had some lame appointment she had to get to, but that he never let her pettiness get to him.

"And he loves me," she added, depositing her plate and cutlery in the dishwasher, and performing a pirouette before disappearing upstairs.

"She's going to phone him again," said Aubrey, a look of ambiguous disgust on his face as he added to a neat ring of mushroom bits encircling the rim of his plate.

Vince announced that his company had won a contract to supply air conditioners to the government of Malta. There would be travel involved. He would have to be gone for two to three weeks at a time.

"How soon?"

"Pretty darn soon, I guess."

"When?"

"Starting this weekend."

Aubrey excused himself from the table and was able to get clean away without clearing his place. Sandra got up and began scrubbing with her fingernail at a spot on the edge of the sink.

"You're upset."

"Why do they call this stainless steel?"

He said some words that had to do with the acquisition of property, the creation of a factory, the training of workers. Her eyes filled, her throat constricted, and in a wave it came, the hot wet blanket enveloping her, the heaves of ragged crying that didn't stop when they usually did, even as she remained mentally calm and amazed at herself. He was saying comforting words, holding her shoulders in the gentle vice of his hands, his cheek sand-papery against hers. Sorry, so sorry. He'd cancel, reschedule. He didn't imagine that the Maltese worked over Easter. Devout, weren't they, as a people? She should count him in.

As quickly as it came the fit was over and she apologized. She thanked him, but didn't say for what. It wasn't only for the comfort of his embrace, the rumblings of tenderness from his throat, but for his sweet lie. Already she was re-aligning her expectations for the holiday to exclude him and to fill his place with whatever might keep the walls in place, a person, an activity, a mantra, a repeated prayer. O Something, bigger than all imagined worlds, let me hang all that I am upon a single peg. Let me be obsessive in my focus again, instead of this, this being a marionette whose parts are held together by wispy threads showing the gaps in my cohesion. Let me be tight, selfish, an inward being.

The last Christmas they all spent together, Faun was two and Sandra was about five months pregnant with Aubrey. Wilomena stopped fussing over inconsequential details—an ornament out of place, the choice of napkins for the table, a postage stamp Bibiana had placed upside-down on the envelope containing her hydro payment—long enough to tell Sandra that she wondered about her sense of timing in getting pregnant again so soon after Daddy had died.

"I beg your pardon?"

When he heard Sandra, Vince stood up from the armchair where he and Faun had been sitting. He held the child in the crook of an elbow, *Yertle the Turtle* dangling by a corner between the pincers of his thumb and forefinger.

"I only meant that your being big with child again is an additional stress on Mother."

"No it's not," said Bibiana. "What nonsense. Don't listen to her."

"Sandra, maybe we should get some air."

"This is Hamilton, Vince, there's no air."

"I only meant, Mother, that another baby would remind you of Daddy, and that it would be hurtful to you."

"Hurtful to you, you mean," said Bibiana.

Sandra took her father for his treatments a few times. Marcel Shea had been a handsome man. His once jet black hair was white and falling out, his lips deflated. Instead of resembling the Dean Martin or Paul Anka of his youth, he looked more like a gaunt Boris Karloff. This had been his own observation and it had made Sandra laugh loudly, startling the woman lying in the bed beside her father, the Cisplatin drip leading into the back of her skeletal hand.

"They're vampires, you know," he said. "All the blood they say they're taking out of me for tests? Lunch! Remember where you heard it first, Bib, my girl."

Sandra hadn't the heart to correct him. He sat propped against pillows, his black reading-glasses halfway down his nose, as he read the tabloid newspaper he liked to buy each day for the colour photographs of young women in bikinis. He refused to change into the hospital gown the nurse wanted him to wear. Sandra had an extra shirt and pair of trousers packed in a small bag for him.

"The anti-nausea drug he's on now should work, but you'd better take a change of clothes, just in case. And his book. And his peppermints if he wants them. Don't forget to have him take out his dentures. Here's their case. You might take some cleaning powder for them. And a change of underwear. I suppose the next step is a disposable diaper. But he did have success this morning."

"For God's sake, Wil, he's not an infant."

"I should really be there with him. I'm sorry, but you just don't—you haven't seen...."

"No, you go to your appointment. We'll be fine. There are still nurses employed at this hospital, aren't there? They haven't all been fired."

After the treatment he had to stop outside the building for a smoke before getting into the car. He wanted to get a drink somewhere. She reminded him that he shouldn't drink alcohol because it dried out his mouth and suppressed his immune system, that he couldn't drive anymore because he had suffered a seizure, that she was his daughter, and that no he hadn't seen her reading the news live at five.

In his last days he was a shrinking eminence sunk into pillows on the couch, the fabric of the furniture now too rough against his skin. He had decided not to continue taking the chemotherapy. The tumour in his brain was growing. He said, No more Dilantin, no more Decadron, I don't care if I lose my appetite, I don't care about swelling or craving or withdrawal. He went off the painkillers, refused morphine, let the pain of the metastases in his femur regain its grip upon his consciousness like a destructive lover one allows, with reluctance but also with excitement, back into one's life.

The bedroom was too dark, he couldn't sleep there anymore. The long couch fit into a three-paned bay window that they left open for him a crack. The stench of the steel smelters wafted in to join his cigarette smoke and the perfume of spilled liquor. Bibiana and Hugh went to live with Bibiana's sister in Toronto. Sandra moved into Wilomena's cramped apartment. Wilomena's spine went out of alignment, but still she refused to leave him.

She got Sandra to put everything non-perishable on the kitchen floor: a plate, bowl, drinking glass, coffee mug, electric kettle, cutlery, instant coffee, whitener, breakfast cereal. Milk and orange juice sat on the floor of the refrigerator, Sandra having removed the three levels of wire rack. Every day she came to cook, to wash the dishes, empty the ashtray, replenish the booze, milk and fruit bowl. Marcel had stopped eating, and Wilomena ate decreasingly as she drank with him to dull her own pain. Sandra put a low telephone table in the middle of the living-room, and her sister knelt there, often falling asleep across a pillow laid upon it. She watched the television, which she never turned off even when the radio was tuned to the news. They drifted in and out of consciousness together. Wilomena talked all hours of the day on the telephone to people who were regularly replaced by increasingly distant contacts when they stopped returning her messages.

Marcel stopped talking. Occasionally the hand not holding a drink would wake to a languid dance. He was oblivious to the television and to Wilomena, who began to buy the items she saw for sale on the shopping channel: jewellery, lounging dresses, a beer-brewing machine, a hand-powered tumble drum for washing clothes one item at a time, a convection cooker, a depilatory jelly, a legal will kit. The couriers got used to having the door opened by a woman on all fours. They would come in and open the packages for her, even though they weren't supposed to. One man even tried to crack her spine, but all he accomplished was the bruising of several of her ribs and the straining of his own back. He asked her out on dates a few times after her father died, but Wilomena always had an excuse.

"You should," said Sandra. "He's very nice, a regular bloke. Gosh, Wil, nobody's saying marry the guy. Just let him buy you dinner and flowers. Get out of this crypt. Introduce yourself to the world again."

"He should never have stopped taking treatment. I should have insisted."

"It was the way he wanted to go."

"He wasn't in his right mind."

"Vince wants me to move in with him. I'm going to say yes. It's time you moved back to your own place. You must miss your privacy. Or, if you don't want to be alone, then stay here when Mother and Hugh come home."

"I won't live here with her. She bailed. Abandoned ship. Spencer I can understand, he couldn't leave his business, it's not a son's place to be a nursemaid, he never had the constitution for suffering, his own or others. But she walked away when Daddy needed her most and I will never forgive him for that."

"Her."

"What?"

"You said, 'him.' 'I'll never forgive him for that.'"

"You'd find fault with a saint, Sandra, you really would."

"It's not Mum you're angry at."

"Oh stop your analysis. You're as bad as that mean doctor on the radio."

For a period of about ten days, while she was still sober enough to be coherent, Wilomena became a regular caller on the dial-in radio shows. She didn't have particularly strong opinions about Quebec sovereignty or the National Energy Policy or gun control laws or the question of what should be done with a budget surplus if there ever was one. Whenever she did get on, she usually repeated the sentiments of those callers she thought had spoken well, and often she would contradict herself from one day to the next. What was important to her was whether or not a caller was reading from a text. She learned how to get past the people screening the calls by giving a précis of a previous caller's argument, rewording it in such a way that it sounded not only original but improved. It was her talent. She reworded the world around her and exposed those unable to speak on their feet. When the call-screeners at the various radio stations began to recognize her voice, she changed her approach and began leaving messages on the programs' answering machines. She kept a small notebook and pencil in the telephone table, recording toll-free numbers, contest questions and the wording of the ubiquitous 'what-is-your-opinion?' prompts.

"Wilomena, you are doing yeoman's duty. You are truly stalwart," said her father one of the last times he communicated a complete thought. He didn't comment upon her participation, via the telephone, in the ongoing, all-inclusive plebiscite, although she always prefaced her comments with, "My father, who is convalescing here at home, agrees with me that...." One host tried to get her to put Marcel on the line. "Oh, no, I'm sorry. I didn't make myself clear. He is quite indisposed."

The day her father died, Sandra arrived to find Wilomena lying on her side trying to assemble an exercise machine that used a person's own body weight to provide resistance for the muscles. The instruction manual was open on the floor behind her and she was trying to fit a socket wrench onto a bolt. A highball glass of rye was sitting canted in the crook of her father's arm. His mouth gaped open, his eyes fixed on the television. She wondered what show had been playing when he died. She vowed to check in the viewing guide as soon as the coroner determined the time of death. What transmission had finally convinced him to let go?

When Sandra was thirteen she accompanied her father to Los Angeles, where there was a vintage car fair he attended every year. They flew to Winnipeg, where they picked up a Jaguar convertible that normally would have been delivered to its new owner by one of his bonded drivers. But his Sandy Girl was becoming a woman, and before the world of men took her away from him, he wanted to show her something of the open road and the big sky.

Wilomena couldn't believe that Sandra and not she was going to the car show. The previous year Marcel had taken

Spencer, who sent Hugh a stack of postcards that became some of his dearest possessions: a white Thunderbird, a red and white Corvette convertible, a black Lincoln Continental town car, the silver-grey Aston Martin from *Goldfinger*. By right of birth order, Wilomena argued, it was her turn to go, given that Hugh was content with his pictures. But she had been asked to work as a nanny for the summer, for the same family she had worked for the year before, the De-Witts, who owned a lodge in the Muskokas, and who liked to be free to sail and attend parties and drive into Toronto to see a show or dine unencumbered by their scrum of four little boys. Wilomena knew how to handle them, knowing intuitively how much leeway to allow and how to negotiate cannily for necessary control. Mr. DeWitt said he liked her because she thought like a man, and he said half-seriously that there would always be a position in the scrap metal business for an astute dealer like her. For the most part she enjoyed taking care of the DeWitt boys. They needed a minimum of supervision. She was there to prevent them from drowning, falling out of trees, becoming lost in the woods, and doing each other physical harm. On rainy days they stayed in their bunks and read comic-books, and Wilomena wrote long letters home.

That summer Sandra sent her sister a postcard from Las Vegas, one in which her face had been inserted in a line of showgirls. "Did you have any idea Pop was such a laff riot?" it read. "We're eating up the miles, aaaaaand...loving it, as Maxwell Smart would say. We'll bring you back a Stude-baker, Wil, whatever that is. Luv U! Sandy Girl."

After that trip, Marcel stopped going to the fair because he stopped dealing in vintage cars. The profit margin was far greater in newer vehicles, ones whose warranties had expired and which had between 50,000 and 100,000 kilo-metres on them. He preferred cash sales, carried a licenced pistol for protection, 'paid the car' $200 for every day that it sat in his possession, writing the money off under a clever umbrella of business expenses, and was audited only once, an experience that almost ruined him, souring him on government in general and tax collectors specifically. And without ever having explained the business of private auto sales to her, Marcel was surprised one day to hear Wilomena telling Hugh why it was better to sell a $35,000 BMW for $18,000 than to hold onto it and wait for someone to pay full price.

"Is it better to eat a doughnut or put it on a shelf and watch it turn into a rock?"

"Eat it!"

"Well, it's the same with Daddy's cars. Every day he holds onto a car he loses money."

"Turns into a rock. Can't drive a rock. Can't eat a rock. Hell on teeth, Wil-mena, right? Right?"

"After a manner of speaking."

"Can't drive a doughnut."

The Christmas of the fire they kept their reminiscences to the well-polished surfaces of their lives. Wilomena had had a roommate, but the woman got married, forcing Wilomena to move to cheaper accommodation, a bachelor apartment with a tiny kitchen and bathroom. Spencer had just opened an electronics store with money from his inheritance. Vince and Sandra were living in Sandy Hill in Ottawa, the house on the wooded lot out in Clayton still an airy dream. Hugh was going to a vocational school, where he learned how to bake, and Bibiana was working in the registrar's office at McMaster. Sandra sat by the fire and listened as they talked about the peculiar enthusiasms filling their lives. They sparked and glowed, alternately challenging, picking at old wounds, then soothing the hurt. It made her think of fireflies winking in the dark.

Hugh brought out his collection of car pictures and spread them over the living-room carpet. He wanted everyone to tell a story about a time their father drove one of the cars. Sandra repeated the one about driving in the Jaguar to Las Vegas and checking into a motel out beyond the glare of the city's core. Marcel had got angry at the desk clerk because the man wanted a hundred-dollar damage deposit in addition to the price for the room.

"Which probably rented by the hour," said Spencer.

The clerk had asked if Sandra really was Marcel's daughter, his skepticism palpable in the hot, antiseptic- smelling office.

"Just give me the bloody key, you bleeping so-and-so," Sandra said, laughing, her approximation of their father's accent, a cross between Michael Caine and Alfred Hitchcock, leaving them breathless with glee. Yes, they agreed, that was Daddy to a tee.

Spencer told the one about Marcel driving him to his figure-skating lesson one morning before dawn, and seeing a distant red glow on the horizon, a light that couldn't have been the sunrise, because they were driving northwest toward the little town where Spencer practised. As they drew closer, the corners of Marcel's mouth betrayed a spreading smile. He was driving a yellow Checker cab, one of the last ones built, cave-like around them, an albatross because the buyer had died before taking possession and his wife had refused to pay for what had been her husband's dream, to own a car he could keep on the road forever, practically live out of, it was so spacious and sturdy. The man had planned to quit his job at the bus station as soon as he had enough money to pay for the car, and rent out the vehicle as a novelty limousine service. He would dress up as a clown for birthday parties, a zombie for Halloween, a snowman for winter, a traditional chauffeur with peaked cap for weddings. He envisioned his wife handling the calls from home and booking the gigs, the various costumes and accoutrements for which he would store in the car's trunk.

"He said, 'Who knows, son, maybe I'll hold onto this one. Can't you see the six of us riding in it on our way to the beach?'"

They all could. But Marcel lost the car soon afterwards when he learned that the taxi had been stolen off the street in Manhattan. That morning, though, under the strange pink sky, the Checker was the car that fit the bizarre nature of the event, which was the burning of the barn-shaped wooden hockey arena where Spencer and a sleepy coterie of little girls traced their figures every Tuesday and Thursday before school. Ever after, Spencer swore he believed in the power of wishful thinking.

"He was only thinking about his lost sleep," said Wilomena.

"God, no, he was thinking, 'Now maybe my eldest son will turn out normal.'"

"Not like me," said Hugh as he gathered his postcards and magazine pictures into a pile.

"No, no, Hughie, that's the last thing Daddy would've thought." Sandra knelt beside him and put an arm around his shoulder. "We haven't finished the stories yet. Mother, it's your turn."

"Marcel and I in a car together? The last time your father and I rode in a car together...would have been in the hearse. Smoothest ride I ever took with the man."

"Alive. You have to say one where he's breathing. Right, Sandra?"

"Oh, shut up, Hugh. This is just about the most idiotic thing. What can this possibly prove? How smart we are and how stupid Daddy was? Really!"

"Wil doesn't want to have to tell."

"You're right. I refuse. Let the dead rest in peace."

"I know why."

"Let it alone, Spencer," said Sandra.

"It's because you can't. There was never a time you were alone with him in one of his beloved automobiles."

"Spencer, I swear."

"And you knew as much about those beauties as he did."

Hugh shuffled through his pile and retrieved a card, a wine-coloured Mercury Marquis, two-doored yet as long as a bus. He stood and held it out to his sister, who was clenched in the attitude of a bull given the sudden gift of awareness. She saw herself beleaguered in the ring, saw her siblings for what they were: a murderous gang of picadors.

She snatched the card from Hugh's hand and shred it in front of his face. She flung the pieces into the fire, and with a stifled shriek picked up the pile of remaining cards.

"I've never been anything to you," she said as she turned and let the glossy images spill from her hands onto the burning log.

In the morning they were startled by the smoke alarm. Sandra, feeding Faun curlicues of bread crust slabbed with butter, was thinking that this was Christmas Eve Day, the best day of the holiday because anticipation kept it pure. She turned toward Spencer standing at the counter, expecting to see smoke coming from the toaster. The alarm was sounding from the hallway leading to the garage. Vince got there first and burned his hand when he touched the door handle. The door darkened as they watched. There was nothing they could do.

"Evacuate!" yelled Spencer.

"What have you done?"

"Nothing, Ma, I swear. The garage is on fire. We have to get out. Somebody get Wil out of bed."

Fire-fighters were able to keep the rest of the house from burning, but smoke damage was extensive. The insurance investigation traced the origin of the blaze to a plastic trash can in the garage. When they asked him if he knew what had happened, Hugh blubbered that he was sorry he made the house catch on fire.

"What do you mean, Hughie? What did you do?"

He said he had sneaked back downstairs after everyone had gone to bed, and had stirred up the ashes with a poker in a futile search for unburned cards. A leaf of ash, a complete card intact like a photographic negative, had wafted out of the grate toward him. He had reached out his hand to catch it, but it had crumbled under his touch.

"Did you take anything out the fireplace, Hugh?" asked Sandra. "Did you put the ashes in the garbage can?"

He looked at Wilomena, who nodded her head. "Go ahead, Hugh," she said.

"Ya, probably I'm pretty sure I did. I'm in bad trouble, right, Sandra?"

"No, Hugh, you're not. It was an accident. It was nobody's fault. Nobody's mad at you."

Sandra said much the same thing to Hugh when she met him coming through the Arrivals portal at Ottawa International. She wasn't angry with him. Faun and Aubrey hugged him extra long, and Ted shook his hand in a manly way. As they waited for his suitcase, Hugh announced to the man beside him that he had flown the airplane all by himself.

"Ah, then you're the one responsible for that landing."

Sandra smiled despite herself. "Were you scared, Hugh? Did someone tell you where to go?"

"Nope, I was double A-OK."

"I can't believe they would do that to you."

"Who?"

"Ma and Wilomena, of course."

"They didn't do a thing. I was flying all by myself. I really surprised myself."

"You surprised everybody, Hughie. I'm just curious. When did they tell you that you were going to be travelling alone?"

"Who?"

"Your mother and your sister."

"I wasn't alone. There was lots of other people."

"I mean without Ma and Wilomena."

"Well, let's see. Ma and me sat in our plane seats and I

got to be beside the window and Wil-mena was standing beside us and people couldn't get by and Ma got out of her seat and then Wil-mena went away and the lady said just make like a seat belt in a car and relax it'll be fun just like a fast ride and it was."

Bibiana and Wilomena called, separately, soon after take-off to tell Sandra that Hugh would be arriving alone.

"The flight is on time, dear, you won't have to stand around waiting."

"What if something had happened, Ma? What if he'd had an anxiety attack or worse?"

"Your brother is a grown man and the flight attendants are trained for emergencies. I don't think your accusatory tone is at all warranted."

"I can't believe you would do this."

"Well, I can't believe you booked us on the same flight. What were you thinking?"

"I was thinking, Wil, that if you had to sit together for an hour you'd be forced to be civil to each other."

Wilomena called again after they got home from the airport with Hugh.

"I'm coming on a later flight."

"You don't have to do that. Ma's not."

"I want to. I feel guilty about leaving Hugh alone on that plane."

"He did fine."

Wilomena wouldn't be deterred. Sandra took down the flight number and arrival time. Faun and Ted volunteered to drive back to the airport a second time. It was no hardship. Ted admitted that he needed the practice. Sandra looked at the boy as if she were meeting him for the first time. She saw that it really wasn't a bother. He and Faun would gladly travel that road to and from the airport all day if need be, if it meant that they could be alone together and pointed toward something purposeful. They would probably pull over by the side of the road and watch the big

107

planes take off and land awhile, just as she and Vince used to do before the children were born.

In many ways it was the best Easter Sandra had ever celebrated. Hugh taught Aubrey how to make doughnuts and crullers. Ted made himself useful driving to the store, chopping wood, and lifting the heavy roast ham in and out of the oven. Without Vince there, the boy didn't try so hard to appear grown up. He was happier with them, he said, than at home. Later, Faun told Sandra that Ted's mother had gone away on a Caribbean cruise with a man she worked with and had only recently begun to date. For the first time Faun asserted a balancing force around her boyfriend, speaking up when she disagreed with something he said, supporting him when his ego needed bolstering. Sandra was aware of a comfortable new separateness in the space between them. Her daughter would not disappear into love's void after all.

Wilomena fussed and cleaned and picked up after them, often creating bigger messes because she couldn't always remember where clothes and kitchen utensils and food items were supposed to go. Sandra pictured her sister home alone in Hamilton in her tiny apartment. Their mother had her circle of friends, including a certain older gentleman she had been seeing casually for a few years; she would be fine on her own. Wilomena needed her family. She needed to feel useful in their midst.

They devoured chocolate and cream-filled pastry, lounged in an air of clockless indolence, wound a stream of conversation like protective gauze around them. They cried at the end of *The Robe*. They played uproarious games of six-person table tennis, nine-ball without pool cues, and something Aubrey called Socialist Monopoly, in which the object was for all the players to work together to break the bank. Sandra calmed them down long enough to read the Easter story aloud. Hugh declared that it was a miracle that the plane didn't crash when he was on it, his innocent statement putting a cooling cap on the evening.

Sandra stayed up a while drinking a glass of red wine in the kitchen. She held particular moments of the day in her mouth before swallowing them. She could not have planned such a day.

She heard something scraping in the living-room and went to investigate. Wilomena, kneeling, was scooping ashes out of the fireplace into a metal bucket.

"There's an easier way to do that, Wil. Just shove it down the little trapdoor." She showed her the lip of the metal plate set flush with the floor beneath the grate, and opened it.

"Well, isn't that a snap," she said as she watched Sandra send the ash from the bucket down the chute. "To think of all that time I spent searching for a suitable container. I finally found this old thing in the garage. I did ask Hugh to look for me, but he was occupied in the kitchen with Aubrey—I just love seeing the two of them together—and you know how much Hugh hates garages. Something must have happened to make him so afraid, don't you think?"

"The fire at Mother's."

"Oh, no, Sandra, he had that fear long before then."

It was as if Wilomena had swung the steel bucket hard against her temple. Sandra turned to look at her sister's face, saw how pleased she was with the swept hearth, all the nasty residue of living and burning hidden away.

"What is it, Sandra. Tell me. What's wrong?"

"Nothing," she said, finally. There was nothing to be done now. The wounds, though still visible, had closed over, the stone been repositioned before the entrance to their sanctuary, the instruments of past pain stowed out of sight. What good would come of accusing her now, after so long? Wilomena remembered that day, all those fiery days, as well as Hugh did, and perhaps less well.

"Sleep well," she said. "Thank you for all you did today, Wil. I'm glad you came."

"Yes, well, you needed help. Obviously."

"What would you like for breakfast? I was thinking about eggs."

"Of course you were. What else would you be thinking about at a time like this? Eggs. If only that were all I had to occupy my mind, my life would be so simple. Yes, dear, eggs would be lovely in the morning."

And so the sisters kissed goodnight and put the darkness of the house between them.

The Girl from the Butts

The trombone sticks its tongue beyond the snack bar counter and back, now far with the long low notes, now quick and short and high. In the floodlit distance pop the last of the day's rifles. Simon varies his tempo to match the retorts until finally his song sputters nameless from the horn. The moon hangs like a target above the butts. He imagines all the competitors standing up from their kneeling or prone positions like a community of New Year's revellers to aim and fire at the late August orb.

Across the field, the shiny pate of Mr. Jerrold, his superior, bobs beside the garbage cans at the kitchen's back entrance. The lids clatter and clang, the rifles pop and crack. He plays a donkey bray that makes the man look up and then retreat inside.

Simon hangs the instrument on a hook on the wall beside the grill. The outdoor lights are extinguished, and for a moment it is quiet on the shooting range. The voice on the loudspeaker announces cumulative scores on this, the fourth day of the week-long shoot. Pakistan is ahead, followed by Ireland and the United States. A dark green military truck, its bed covered by a canvas canopy, drives up the middle of the range. He pours himself a cup of coffee, takes a sip, grimaces, and then brings two cases of pop forward from the storage-room. The truck pulls up outside his window, and soon a happy throng is milling restlessly at the counter.

He takes orders for soft drinks and candy, making change, drawing energy from the onslaught. They know not to order the coffee.

He directs his smile at a girl in a white halter-top. She has sun-coffeed skin, long thick Black Forest hair brushed straight back from the forehead, aching dimples, full lips, deep chocolate eyes.

"Hey, Marita. Was it a good day today?"

She smiles and blushes, looking down and then up again. "It was okay, I guess. I like working outside. We have fun." She glances to either side of her for confirmation.

A boy standing behind her moves closer and says, "Better believe it. Hey, Sime...."

He continues to gaze at Marita.

"...you should come out and see us sometime. Maybe Marita will decide to sunbathe *au naturel* again."

"Joey!" Marita's eyes flash with outrage and delight, and she whirls and punches the sunburnt boy in the arm. She glances back at Simon to register his response. "I never did."

"What exactly *do* you do out there?"

"Oh, that's classified," says Joey, rubbing his bicep, "and very steamy."

"We take the target down, we record the score and we put up a new one," says another voice.

"Nadine! You're so one-dimensional."

After they have been served and are climbing back into the truck for the ride home into Ottawa, Marita returns to the counter.

"My sister wanted me to check again about Saturday night."

"We'll be there," he says. "I told the band this was a special gig."

"She's so nervous."

"How about you?"

"She put us in yellow. I can live with yellow, I suppose. But we had the rehearsal last night. I couldn't believe it. My father kept interrupting the minister with suggestions about the wording of the ceremony and about how long it should take him and Trish to come down the aisle."

"He just wants it to click."

"You don't know him. He has to control everything."

"What do I do if he wants to direct the band?"

"Let him," she says, making him laugh. "Just...."

"Just what?"

"You don't have to say anything about this place. Let's just say that it's not one of his favourite subjects."

"Okay. So, Macdonald Room, seven o'clock."

"Right. Thank you for doing this on such short notice. You won't let me down, will you, Simon?"

How could he ever? He watches her climb into the back of the truck and sit nearest the opening. She waves as they drive away.

He is still floating as he closes up for the night. He hits hard ground when the telephone rings. 'Coward,' he thinks. Only one person ever phones the shack.

"Miller. You're on pots starting tomorrow morning."

"And a pleasant good evening to you, too, Mr. Jerrold."

"Save it. Eight to ten. Then I need you to show the new guy what's what."

"The new guy."

"He's taking over for you. Show him where everything's kept, how the cash works, how to clean the grill. All that."

His full heart shrivels. He can only imagine what he has done to deserve this.

That night he lies awake until late. His army-brat roommates, the three Baby Cretins from Oromocto, don't respond to his repeated request that they turn off their music. He takes their machine from them and hides it on the bunkhouse roof. They are too drunk to get off their beds to look for it. At two in the morning he awakes to the sound of retching followed by an embarrassed snickering beside his bed. He throws off the blanket, grabs a handful of shirt and hair, and marches the perpetrator into the washroom, where he splashes cold water on the boy and then introduces him to the mop and bucket.

"Over there," he directs. "You missed a spot."

He leads the boy back to bed and covers him up.

At six he gets up, smooths the sheet and the grey blanket, shaves half-heartedly at the washroom's line of stainless steel troughs, dons a set of whites and walks across the wet grass and gravel to the kitchen. He leans his spine against the corner of the building and slides into a squat. The first smell of frying bacon wafts brazenly through the open door.

As the butts truck rounds the corner, he stands up, tucking his shirt back into the kitchen uniform's baggy pants. He breaks into a sprint behind the vehicle, catching the attention of most of the half-awake eyes in the back.

"Hey! Get him to stop. Stop the truck for a sec," he calls.

"Somebody fall out again?" says the driver, leaning out his window.

Simon steps up onto the bumper. Marita is sitting near the back again. She says hello as if this were a scheduled stop and he did this every day.

He says, "I was wondering...I mean if you're not...doing anything after...work, maybe we could...I don't know... take in a movie."

"What did he say?"

"He's asking her out on a date."

"Can we get a move-on, here?" says the driver. "I got another pick-up in ten minutes."

"I don't care if we sit here all day, long's we get paid."

"Hey, Sime, great duds. You the Dickie Dee man or what?"

Marita says, "I have to go to a bridal shower for Trish tonight. I have to host it, actually."

"Oh. Well."

"He's the Man from Glad! Simone, you coming out to see our butts, or what?"

"If there was any way I could get out of it."

He takes a courage breath. "Do you get a break sometime? I could meet you for lunch."

"Some enchanted evening, you will meet a strangler!"

"Go ahead, kiss dee girl!"

She holds up a thermos bottle. "We have to stay out all day. You're welcome to try and come out there, but I don't know, they're pretty strict about people just strolling around the range. I mean, you could try."

"All right. I will."

He steps down and the truck pulls away.

"Bye, Simon!"

"See you, Mister Miller!"

"Well, I think he's kinda cute. Marita, if you don't want him...."

"He's too old for her. What's he doing working in a place like this, anyway?"

"I heard he used to play in an orchestra."

"I think it's so romantic."

He wanders around the base until it is time for work. Just inside the door to the kitchen two of the Baby Cretins are making green salads for lunch. They wear black hairnets. One hacks at pieces of carrot, red pepper, celery, mushroom and tomato with a large blade on a wooden chopping-board. The other boy arranges the vegetables with a jeweller's precision on beds of green.

"Watch this, man," he says, his eyes flashing from behind thick bangs that refuse to be constrained. "Watch what happens when I turn the bowl. It's just like one of them things you look through."

Sodden pancakes are floating in Simon's sink. He removes them to the garbage can, then scrapes out the pots. He lets out the grey dishwater, shakes out the trap, replaces it, scrubs down the sides with a stiff brush, and fills the sink anew with soap and the hottest water he can stand. Across the room, a boy with a blank look on his face loads plates onto the conveyor belt that takes them through the washing and drying machine. At the other end, the boy who was sick during the night and is still looking green removes them from the machine and stacks them. The head cook mutters in hushed conference with one of the seconds.

"If he does it again, you come get me, no matter where

I'm at or what I'm after doing."

"Why don't you just cook the things a little longer?"

"They're fully Jesus cooked! Are you changing sides on me now, Norman? Because you can just plain go piss into the wind."

"He's going to order the same thing tomorrow."

"And he'll get more of the sweet-Joseph-and-Mary-Mother-of-God same. I don't care who the bastard is or what his bleeding rank."

"Maybe you gentlemen could head him off before he dumps his breakfast into my wash water."

"And who's this listening in on private conversations now? Oh, excuse me, it's the Maestro. Slumming it, are we?"

"Morning, Patrick."

"You know, I gots me eye on you, boyo. Do a good job on the ribs pan this after lunch and I'll make you me personal aide-de-camp.

He grins, shrugs his shoulders against Paddy's laughter and turns back to the sink. As he rinses down the remaining suds and hangs the last of the pots, he thinks about Marita cloistered all day in her concrete bunker beneath the targets.

Mid-morning, Mr. Jerrold finds him having coffee with the waitresses in the dining-hall. A young man accompanies the manager.

"This here's Wendell. Wendell, Miller. He'll show you the operation. Any questions, ask him. Got it?"

"Yes, Uncle Phil. I mean, sir."

"I don't want to hear a word from anybody about you. Got it?"

"Yes sir, you bet, no probs."

"For crying out loud."

Wendell proves to be competent though anxious and overly eager to please. Simon shows him how to balance the cash, replace the register tape and prepare the grill with vegetable oil and the cleaning stone. He tells him how big a cash float he should have, how many hamburgers and hotdogs to take out of the freezer each morning, and when to expect lineups during the day.

"Whatever you do, never re-heat the previous day's coffee."

"Why would I do that?"

"Exactly. You're on your own, then."

After the lunchtime cleanup, he returns to see how the lad is doing. Tenzing, one of the Gurkhas, is ahead of six other people waiting restlessly in line.

"I'm sorry, could you say that again? I didn't quite make out...."

"Ahmboogera! Ahmboogera!

Simon goes into the storeroom and comes out with a bottle of red wine and a long sourdough baguette. "Hamburgers, Wendell. You'll need eighteen of them. It'll take a package and a half."

The little soldier turns to him. "Where you went, Mirrer? Why you not working here any soon?"

"I've been promoted. I'm now the kitchen's hygiene control officer."

"Ah, high position, more cash bucks maybe."

"Would that it were true."

"This new guy, little too sillious. Gotta righten up, like you. Pray some music, maybe."

"Music hath charms, as they say."

"Ah, yes, quotation. This I have learning in school. 'Music have chums to smooth a sewage bees.' Sometime we praying together, you and me. This after day, yes fine?"

They agree to get together in the evening.

On his way out to the butts, as he walks along the edge of the firing area, he is stopped by a military policeman.

"Where are you headed, my friend?" The MP raises his eyebrows at the bulging plastic grocery bag he is carrying.

"I'm meeting someone for lunch. She works out there in

the butts."

"Pass."

But when he starts walking again the man puts out his arm as a barrier.

"As in show it to me, darling."

"What if I don't have one?"

"Then this is where you turn around."

"But I'm a civilian employee of the base."

"I don't care if you're the Minister of Defence. Nobody's out here without a pass."

"How about my band plays for free at your funeral?"

The big man darkens. Simon turns and walks back the way he came.

He gets through the supper shift without breaking anything or provoking anyone to violence. When Tenzing shows up after supper with his banjo, he finds Simon stewing in self-pity. They sit together on steel chairs behind the bunkhouse and the marksman plays, "Soldier's Joy," "Rocky Mountain Breakdown" and "The Ballad of New Orleans." To reciprocate, Simon plays, "Stardust," the theme from *Deliverance* and a selection from *Brigadoon*. Then Tenzing plays a quiet, lilting tune from his homeland. Simon asks him to play it again. Tenzing wipes his eyes with the back of his hand and obliges him, and later he shows Simon pictures of his wife and daughters. The full moon pops above the butts again before nightfall. As their last number they play, "Amazing Grace." They complement each other and are so absorbed by the song's enduring echoes that the truck carrying the butts gang speeds by before he has a chance to notice. He stops in the middle of, "blind but now I see" and gazes longingly at the twin red lights fading in the fine white dust of the base road.

Tenzing stops picking and sings, "Go-hum, go-hum, go-hum wiz Bunny Jeans."

"I wish, Moe. Oh, how I wish."

"There are many beautifuls girl putting up with new

targets. Think one is maybe steal Mirrer heart."

"I can't even get close to her. They won't give me clearance to step onto the range."

"My people got saying when jungle get really thick: What else you gonna put there? Sandy dunes? Pucking lot?"

"What are you trying to say, Moe?"

"You get lost in jungle, sit down you asp and staying put. Something finding you. Maybe such-potty, maybe snek."

Perhaps because it is too quiet, the Baby Cretins having made their way into Ottawa and across the river to Hull, where they can get into bars and don't have to return until Saturday at dawn, he can't sleep again. He has begged off coming into town to stay the weekend as he usually does with his mother, citing as his excuse the fact that the competition runs until Sunday, making his services indispensable beginning early in the morning. He doesn't correct her belief that he is helping to prepare culinary masterpieces under the direction of one of the military's finest chefs. It is a little lie, he tells himself, not sure whether he tends it for her benefit or his.

He needs no security clearance to be out on the rifle range after the lights have been shut off. As he approaches the butts the turf embankment looms like a long, pocked burial mound. He has to walk to the rightmost limit of its length to find a way down into the bunkers, a line of shallow concrete alcoves set into the back of the hill, each opening onto a common corridor and each with a target positioned above. A gunmetal box with one green and one red light mounted on the wall tells the keeper when to venture up the ladder and when to stay beneath the overhang. Large thin cardboard sleeves holding fresh targets lean in each cubicle. The only other item common to each space is a three-legged wooden stool.

He is surprised to see no refuse strewn about, no unrolled condoms, no cast-off panties or bottles of sun-block, not even a portable recliner. If the rumoured orgies do take place here in this hidden world that passes the day bombarded by design, then their carnival trappings are erected and torn down with a stark and traceless precision. He is content to have seen where Marita chooses to work. She and he share this in common, at least: they both replace other people's messy creations with a clean and shiny surface. But the subterranean confinement, the drabness and the ever-present danger of this place is unsettling in a way that the kitchen, for all its wet heat and warring odours and petty people, never is, and he feels an aspect of his infatuation shift out of true.

It shifts back when he sees her the next evening at the reception in the hotel. First the bride and groom dance, then the bride's father cuts in and the floor fills with couples relieved to be up and moving about after the food and the speeches. Because it is raining outside, the band—trombone, trumpet, electric guitar, keyboard and drums—chooses to play three on a theme. The mother of the bride, sensing bad luck, suggests something with a rainbow in it, and so they play the one that usually caps the evening. Everyone applauds the choice. After 40 minutes, he announces a short break and is emptying his spit valve when Marita strides across the room toward him.

"I thought you were coming out to see me today."

"Is that like a Mae West invite? Come on out to the butts, big boy. Come out and see me sometime. Bring your ...rifle." Can she tell that he can't breathe? Can she feel the earthquake centred in his chest?

"May Who?"

"I really did try to make it out there." He tells her about his planned picnic and the impassable meathead.

"I'm sorry. Promise me you'll try again?" He promises. "Will you dance with me?"

"I happen to know that the band is on a break. Pretty strong union."

"Then sing to me. I won't tell anyone that you performed while dancing on your break."

He hums a little of "Paper Moon" into her fragrant hair as he holds her soft against him, the two of them alone in the middle of the dance floor, witnessed by happy, sleepy, dressed-up people, and she tells him that it has been a long summer. The boy she has been seeing at school is away looking for uranium in northern Saskatchewan. They have exchanged a few letters, but the boy's tone has grown less and less intimate. All he writes about are the black flies and the tedium and the odd characters he works with. She isn't sure what their relationship amounts to anymore. She asks him if he has ever been in that situation with a girl.

"Has it ever been that one minute you're thinking about forever with a person and the next you can't remember what they look like?"

Yes, he says, he knows that moment, that shift very well.

"Have you ever been married?"

"Almost," he admits. "Twice, to the same girl. She gave up waiting."

"Waiting for you to ask her."

"Waiting for me to get serious."

"Have you ever told a lie and kept it going so that you could just be yourself?"

"I've done that," he says.

"If it doesn't hurt anyone, then it's all right, don't you think?"

He is about to say, 'Yes, it is the most natural thing in the world to save people from disappointment by allowing them to continue to believe what they want to believe about you,' and on the heels of that thought, in the same breath, he prepares to say, 'I'm falling in love with you, Marita—no, I've already fallen in love with you,' when a loud voice interjects,

"Would the young lady who kidnapped our illustrious leader please return him to the stage? We will gladly pay any ransom under $5."

They hang on at arm's length for a beat longer, her eyes saying, 'What? What is it?' and then she blushes and shoos him back to the band. From all around them come claps and playful hoots and whistles.

All during the final set he plays mechanically while keeping her in his sights. It stiffens him to do so, hollowing out and flattening his sound, so that his trumpeter moves to the front of the stage nearer the microphone, and he takes a step back. The only conduit he has to communicate his feelings now are his eyes, and for a while she maintains the connection. His look is so fierce and his playing so discernibly off that she looks away and doesn't look back until the trumpet player thanks everyone for a great evening and wishes them safe passage home. The lights go up and from across the room she smiles and mouths, 'See you tomorrow,' pointing her finger at him, firing and then blowing away the smoke. He motions to her to wait for him, but she has already turned toward the door.

A woman in a tight blue dress says, "Marita's never mentioned you. Excuse me? Hello-o."

"Hello?"

"Now, Marita would have told her mother about someone like you, sir."

"Yes. Thank you very much. Wonderful evening."

"You must work in her section, then."

"I'm sorry. Pardon me?"

"Marita's section. You work together."

"That's right."

"You're helping with the genome mapping project, then."

"I help with the cooking."

"Cooking? I'm sorry, I don't quite understand. You do work with Marita, don't you?"

"Same place, different ends of the range. We're both in the support area, you might say. I give them something to shoot with; she gives them something to shoot at."

"Range? What on earth are you talking about?"

"Would you excuse me, ma'am? I'd like to say goodbye to her." But by then Marita is nowhere to be seen.

The next afternoon he is jamming with Tenzing behind the bunkhouse when a sleek silver car drives out beyond the firing line and stops. A tall man in a tailored grey suit gets out, leaving the door of the car open and strides purposefully in the direction of the butts. Simon has seen that walk before. He puts down his trombone and walks slowly toward the rifle range, now silent but for the broadcast exhortations that the man remove himself from the line of fire. Others outside in the sun after the rainy night—the Baby Cretins in the process of shaving their heads, Norman the second cook playing the harmonica, Paddy revising the breakfast menu, two waitresses smoking and flipping through glossy magazines—turn their attention to the car.

As the two figures come into focus Marita breaks free of her father's hold on her wrist and runs ahead sobbing. She doesn't look at Simon as she ducks into the car, although he comes close enough for her to see him. Calling out, 'I'm sorry, forgive me, please,' won't change the outcome. She will be driven home in disgrace, and if she is lucky she'll still be able to work for a few weeks in the NRC laboratory where her father had arranged a job for her at the beginning of the summer. For Simon to say at this moment of defeat, 'I love you, Marita,' won't help her father understand why she has chosen a menial job over one offering such promise for her education and career. Nor will it help her to understand why her father has chosen to bring her childhood to an abrupt close in such a theatre of humiliation as this.

While Simon stands mute watching her being driven away, he feels the entire establishment fold like a cardboard game around him, and he knows that before the day is out he'll be giving Mr. Jerrold his notice.

The New Road

The side road off the highway used to run close behind each little cottage. It was a double track etched by the wheels of the cars, with a ridge of grass running down the middle. The cars would inch along carefully, for no-one knew what tow-headed toddler, dotted with itch lotion and clad only in a diaper, was going to run out from behind a trailer. The chrome-trimmed cars, wide and long, fin-tailed, loaded inside and out, bellying low over the grassy track, moved gingerly down dips and around rocks, their windows rolled down with kids hanging out to see who had already arrived at the lake. Who was there to play with, to spy on from a distance, to meet for the first time, to re-discover after ten months—an eternity!—apart in different cities or different neighbourhoods in winter? Look who's up, see what they're having for supper, said those arriving, for they could count the place settings through the screened kitchen windows as they drove past.

On calm days the parents rowed or canoed to get milk at the little store at the far end of the bay, or in the evenings, with cricket song shunting the heat from the day, the children walked in bare feet along the edge of the highway, five steps along the blacktop, four on the gravel shoulder, to let a car speed past or their soles cool. Half-clad, shins charted with scratches and scabs and mosquito bites, mouths ringed sweet with orange melt, they gobbled their loot even before reaching the side road, a few naked popsicle sticks closer to the thousand they needed to win a trip around the world. But the second reel of summer always wound itself out faster than the first, and they fed their small treasure of tongue depressors to the giant midsummer bonfire. Besides, they said, they were sick of trudging all the way up to the store, where the owner had yelled at them never to come in again without their shoes on, they left such sticky shadows of themselves on her clean linoleum.

Each year the new cars got better suspensions and the children wanted more diversion, the lake contributing to a monotony that made them listless and their parents edgy. The traffic in and out increased at all hours, and finally, after letting the debate subside over the Labour Day weekend and flare up again over the Victoria Day holiday, while in co-operative clots they helped each other slide their docks and rafts and intake lines into the cold water of the benign lake, they decided to build a new road, a paved one removed a good distance from the cottages. They cut connecting lanes, dug wells and septic systems, and jacked up their cottages to put in insulated basements. Now they could come and go without disturbing each other, and stay the year round if they wanted to. They let the dirt track grow over, absorbing it into their backyards where new fences and clotheslines and hedges marked property lines. The cottagers built guest cabins and boat sheds, their children growing apace with the resale price of their properties. Lord knows, they needed the extra room.

The Fosters were one of the few families on the beach who did not own property there. For the past few years they had rented a tiny blue cottage owned by the Sinclairs. The blue cottage was one in which Mrs. Foster had summered as a girl. She convinced her husband to spend his two weeks of vacation there and then let her stay another two weeks alone with the boy and the girl after he went back to work Monday to Friday. The cottage had electricity but no heat or running water, and they had to use an ancient outhouse that smelled so bad they took to breathing through a perfumed handkerchief whenever they had to go.

When it rained they caught the drips in chipped white enamel bowls stained with rust. The four of them sat around an oilcloth-covered table built into the corner of the kitchen and there they played Hearts. One evening Jeffery tried to go for control but failed by one, and his father laughed at him so heartlessly that the boy fled the table. He ran out, through the rain and wet foliage, toward the highway, not along the newly built paved road but following the old track, and as he passed he slapped the side of each cottage with the flat of his hand. He knew everyone inside, and didn't care if he was disturbing them, he felt so restless and cooped up. He felt like crying like a baby over the lost hand of cards and also like laughing back at his father, laughing so madly and derisively as to shrivel the man to dust. He felt like crawling into a culvert and waiting there for three weeks until they gave up looking for him and pronounced him dead.

By the time he reached the highway his anger was spent, but he would not let himself drift back, not yet. His sister Essie would say something singsong to make him blush and burst and want to wrap his hands around her chicken neck, and his father would laugh again, and his mother would scold and fuss him dry with a towel still wet from the day before when there had been sun and for hours they had swum like otters. He looked west: the highway in that direction curved around the lake, past the store that sold candy, dew worms, carved figurines of fishermen hooking themselves by the seat of their pants, and sweatshirts with the name of the lake imprinted on them, and on to the town where his mother bought groceries. East was the way home, the hot city with its brittle brown lawns. These three directions he did not want to go: back to the cramped blue hut with its leaky roof and sagging cots, ahead into the two-street town, or in retreat home to the city.

Tomorrow his father would drive away to his job and return to the lake only twice, once on Friday night, late, his headlights cutting like lasers through the cracks in the cottage wall, waking them, and again the following Friday to spend the last weekend with them before they packed to go home. Jeffery was ashamed that they could afford only a few weeks in the old rented shack. He wished they owned a cottage of their own. Then he would not have to walk past the Sinclairs' kitchen window twice a day on his way to fill the bucket with water from the hand pump.

On his way to the pump he looked to see if Deanna Sinclair was there. He flipped his head sideways and back so that his long blond hair uncovered his eyes and then settled low again over his forehead. Deanna at thirteen had been as tall and curvy as she would ever be, and here she was already seventeen. She had clear skin, straight teeth, a practical face that hid little, slim long legs and full breasts. One night while they sat on the beach and watched a bonfire burn down to holes of red light in the sand, she whispered in his ear. She said that she was bored and he had replied that he was sorry, he didn't know that he was supposed to be her entertainment, and had begun to stand, wiping the sand from his bare legs, which were long and slender and finely haired. She asked him what he was running away from all the time. "Go ahead," she said, "there's only the two of us here," and he said, "Go ahead and what?" "Go ahead and tell me, what did you think I meant?" "I didn't think you meant anything," he said, not wanting to walk back to his musty mattress and sleeping-bag.

Whenever they played cards, he positioned himself next to Deanna, pressing his bare thigh against hers, passing her low cards if they were playing Hearts or, if he felt she was ignoring him, the Queen of Spades, and she would reach under the table and dig her long nails into his skin. There were Deanna and her two sisters, Belle and Betina; he and Essie; Brenda Tighe, whose father was an admiral; the Stronberg tribe of seven; and Margaret McGarry, who watched him with a sly, smirking intelligence that told him she saw him being reeled in by Deanna and wasn't he the fool.

The conversation always came round to Johnstone's, a campground five miles around the lake on the way to town, a place with few trees where people came with trailers and recreational vehicles. The Johnstones let a travelling carnival set up in one of their meadows for a week each summer as a diversion for the campers. There was a Ferris wheel and a Tilt-a-Whirl and a giant waterslide and a row of games of chance. The carneys who operated the rides and manned the games were sunburned, hard-looking young men with impenetrable, sullen eyes, grease in their hair and on the backs of their hands, and hand-rolled cigarettes stuck behind their ears.

By the time the girls were old enough to climb into cars and trucks with boys, they already knew their way around Johnstone's. The local boys who arrived to pick them up, in cars and pickup trucks and outboard motorboats, resembled the ones who ran the amusement park, but were younger and cleaner looking. The campground was the great flame they were drawn to every night that the carnival was there. Around the rides and the games the girls built an entire world of intrigue and romance, for every summer there were two or three new boys whose hard, impassive faces and wiry bodies spoke of a brand of excitement entirely missing from the beach, its row of dully familiar cottages, the hot stifling tar of the newly laid road, the unremarkable, all too subtle variance of the wind and water.

Jeffery watched Deanna climb into B.J. Blondell's truck one evening after dark when the mosquitoes seemed to rise like smoke from the grass and the fireflies winked at him. He let a barrage of self-pitying questions volley inside his head: Why had his father left them stranded without a car? Why wasn't he as attractive as the greasers who operated the amusement rides? Why wouldn't Deanna let him take her in his canoe to the secluded diving rock on the other side of the lake? When he suggested they do just that, one brooding, low-lidded day when grey clouds scudded just out of reach of the pines' crowns, piling into each other, she had rolled her eyes at him through the screendoor. She invited him in, "to play cards or something." It was going to rain, didn't he know that? It was too cold for swimming.

"Who's that, Dee?" her mother called from one of the curtained-off bedrooms at the rear of the cottage.

"Just Jeffery," she said. Then, "You coming in or not?"

He came in, sunk down into their soft chesterfield, his knees level with his chin, and let himself be corralled. What he wanted was to worship her some place far away from who they were here, family-stricken, polite, doomed. He wanted to look at her there, in a suspension of heat and moving air while she stretched out on the bone-dry outcrop that rose like the back of a brown bear climbing from the water on the far shore, and watch her arch and turn with closed eyes and parted lips from side to side, inviting the sun.

From out on the lake the crescent of golden sand looks like a dimple or a scar in the wide cheek of the bay. Along the beach stand tall red pines shading the plywood-walled cottages, some stained rust, some painted robin's-egg blue, some the military green of a bruise. When the lake was glass Jeffery gathered flat stones and stood at the water's edge where the sand had the feel of wet velvet between his toes. There he whipped the disks sidearm, putting on each one a backspin with his index finger so that it would touch down like a whizzing saucer and skip forming a chain of splashes that blended into a seamless archipelago, curving, slowing, sinking away. After spending each batch of stones, he turned and hunted for more, higher on the beach where the best ones lay buried in strata near the roots of the tall pines.

He was doing this one day when Margaret McGarry came from behind him and dug her strong fingers into his unprotected sides, jolting more than tickling him. Then she ran away from him into the water, dove like a sleek seal and stroked a smooth crawl out to the Sinclairs' raft. He dropped the handful of skippers he was holding, shucked off his shirt and splashed in after her. She was lying on her back when he reached the raft, her fat thighs masking bone and muscle, giving her legs the look of appendages useless out of the water. He hauled himself up in one motion, but she didn't look up. He stood over her.

"You're dripping on me."

"I can do better than that."

"Oh, you can, can you?"

Like a dog he shook his hair at her, then sat with his legs straight out in front of him, leaning back slightly on his arms, which he locked at the elbow and tensed to accentuate his triceps.

"If I can get the car tonight, would you like to go to Johnstone's?" she said. "Maybe, after, we could drive up to the mountain."

Because it hadn't been his idea, and because this was the only way he could go anywhere, by getting rides with others, he let her think he was making up his mind. She put him off-balance because she was more intelligent than he was and because she so unguardedly wanted to love him. She bothered him the same way he had felt strangely aroused once when wrestling in gym class. He had been matched with a boy shorter but heavier than he, and although he moved quickly he could not put solid holds on the boy. The more he went after his opponent the more the boy slipped out from beneath him, and a kind of desire in him grew. He wanted to employ his whole body to stop this boy from moving, to hold him still and limb-locked on the dense foam rubber mat. He wished that if he held Margaret McGarry in that full body embrace she would resist as urgently as had that boy. If he could overpower her, pour all the pent-up, jittery spume of his agitation into those muscles, let her fight him, try to push him off, then she might be his vent. She might drain him of his uneasiness so that when he was with Deanna she would sense his newly found composure, the words he chose and his gestures right, and be drawn to him. But he knew Margaret would never fight him.

"Your sweetheart will be there," she said.

"She's not my sweetheart."

"You wish she was."

"And what made you so wise all of a sudden?"

"All of a sudden! All of a sudden!" she cried, rising too quickly for him to react, rolling him over the side of the raft.

When his head broke the surface, she finished, saying, "I've been wise to you since we were eleven."

"I'll go to Johnstone's with you. Only, we stay together. This isn't some set-up where you find some grease-monkey and leave me to walk home."

He couldn't tell from her face, he was too mummified in his own concerns, but she almost cried then, for the joy of what he'd said, that he wanted them to be together the whole evening, and for the absurdity that she would ever abandon him.

She said she would pick him up. He didn't want the Sinclairs to see him getting into a car with her, and so he said that he would walk down the new road to the driveway leading to her family's cottage and wait for her there. He told his mother that a bunch of them were going to the campground that evening, and that he wasn't sure who was driving. He would be sure not to get into a car driven by anyone who had been drinking, he added, thinking that this would address her apprehension, which it did, but only to heighten it. He was to call Blondell's, the motel-style cottages at the end of the road, if he got himself stuck, and ask them to pass the message on to Mrs. Sinclair, and she would send someone out to Johnstone's to get him.

"I'm so glad you're going out for a change, Jeff," said his mother, "it'll take you out of yourself."

131

The McGarry cottage was seven away from the Fosters' blue rental, closer to the end of the bay and the highway. When he got there he knocked on the door of their new sleeping-cabin, where Margaret was staying alone. It had room for a bed, chair and desk, and stood close to the new road like a tiny gatehouse or one of the more substantial shelters rural children used while waiting for the schoolbus in winter-time. She opened at the sound of his knock as if she had been waiting for it, and did nothing to hide her pleasure at seeing him standing there. She said she had to tell her mother she was going, that he could wait there or in the car, an old Volkswagen Beetle, which was parked beside the cabin. "Whatever tickles your fancy," she said. He chose to wait out of sight. Clothes lay strewn about the room and the bed was unmade. A heavy musk perfume hung over everything.

She asked him if he would like to drive. He wanted to be seen driving into the campground, but didn't know how to operate the standard transmission, and so he slouched in the passenger seat instead. He watched Margaret's right hand work the stick-shift in concert with her left foot on the clutch and right working the accelerator, and tried to understand the rhythm of the gears, the positioning of the stick, the sound the engine made in transition from one stage to the next. He would have to try it himself, he concluded. It must be like playing piano or violin, he imagined, too complicated to learn simply by watching. Margaret was saying something about her brother, who was spending the summer in the army reserves. He could tell that she was only talking to ease the tension that silence brought into the car. She wasn't normally one to chatter.

His stomach was beginning to clutch and dance because he wasn't looking out the window. He knew how far they were along the highway simply by feel, he had travelled that stretch so many times. He wanted to tell Margaret something noble before they got to the campground, that he admired her for the way she drove so expertly, hardly touching the brake, letting the engine slow and accelerate the car so smoothly, or for the thick books she read so effortlessly, or for the way she had swum across the lake and back without stopping, her father rowing patiently behind her. But to praise her would be to acknowledge that he could do none of these things, and the thought made him feel all the tighter and smaller and more insignificantly *himself*.

The carnival area at Johnstone's was flooded with light. Margaret pulled off the highway and into a grassy area where a young boy with a flashlight had directed her to park. Through a space between the bumper-car ride and the ticket kiosk, Jeff could see some of the campers' trailers at the edge of the meadow where the amusements had been erected. No-one camped here to appreciate the serenity of the lake and its surroundings. There may have been tents hidden at a distance among the trees, but he doubted it. The focus of the carnival was a large, open-sided beer tent from which rock music and talk and laughter emanated. Many of those seated at picnic tables inside the dark tent looked to be his age or younger. Deanna was there sitting with her sisters and three darkly clad boys.

She looked directly at him. When he raised his hand hello, she turned her head away and took a sip of her beer. His stomach felt as if she were emptying it as she drank, leaving a tight vacuum.

They wandered for a while and then he told Margaret that he wanted to leave.

"We just got here."

"You didn't really want to go on the rides, did you? They're the same ones every year."

"No, I guess not," she said. She slid her hand into his. "I don't care where we go."

He left his hand there. "Not back to the lake."

"The Look-off, then," she decided for both of them.

The "Mountain," all of 300 feet high, looked over the lake to similar hills on the other side of a valley. They drove as close to the top as the road could reach and parked in one of the look-off spots, the nose of the car close to a steel guardrail. He had hiked up here before, along a footpath that began at the highway and continued past the look-off to the summit and beyond. Being suddenly there in the dark without having had to work, his breathing regular, mouth moist, skin dry, the surface of the lake spread below like a fish shimmering under a half-moon, firelight winking in a broken necklace along the beaches, made it seem unreal. It felt as if he could reach out his hand and scoop up all the water in a single gesture.

He could hear but not see Johnstone's campground. Margaret was looking straight ahead of her and he knew she was aware of him looking at her. Everything about her was full, substantial, her round, pretty face, her blunt haircut, her plump shoulders and thighs and breasts. He wondered if he could lift her, felt the urge to do so, to jam one of his shoulders into her crotch, drape her over his back and straighten into the fireman's lift, powering up with his legs. She was not much shorter than he and was as heavy, he figured. He would be lifting himself. He needed something. He tried to think about lifting Deanna that way, but it wasn't right. She would never agree to it. Deanna was the kind of girl you carried cradled light in your arms, her arms encircling your neck, her head cushioned on your shoulder, her legs scissoring once, twice, again, toes pointing the way. The Deanna Sinclair of his mind, he saw, was as unreal as the glinting metal lake spread before him.

The lake itself, the brief time in the tiny cottage, the indulgence of solitude, boredom and longing, were already fading like the old side road now grassed over, sectioned, built upon, its blunted edges perceptible only at a squint.

"I've thought about you, about being up here with you," said Margaret, who was looking at him now as he stared up

134

at the ladle moon. He turned and saw a spot on her neck pulsing.

As he kissed her, he felt a part of him disappearing and another part, newly tarred, blatant, taking shape. He kissed awkwardly, open-mouthed, hungrily. They left the car. She took his hand and they walked across the road and up the trail until the trees hid them, and they lay down entwined on the dry, spongy ground. He tore at her belt and the zipper of her jeans, and he buried his face and his hands in every part of her.

Afterwards, he asked if he might drive the car back, and on one of the more level side roads she gave him a lesson. He drove, haltingly, improving as he went, all the way in, past the Sinclairs and right to the door of the little blue cottage. She said it was all right: she was protected and the clutch wasn't burnt out.

"Are you sure?"

"Yes," she said, "it works fine."

"I meant...."

"Don't worry." She smiled and kissed him.

He got out and in the light cast by the Beetle as it backed away he glimpsed movement in the bushes. The top of the outhouse was wobbling. He went down the path and found his father struggling with the structure. He still had his city clothes on but had removed his jacket and tie. He stood in a half-squat embracing one corner with the whole thing tilted back against his shoulder. Jeffery could see it was too heavy for him and he positioned himself at the opposite corner.

"Your mother read the Riot Act. Can you imagine? No sleep until this is done."

"It is pretty bad," said Jeffery as they waltzed the outhouse away from the hole, releasing the smell at its most foul.

"A new crapper or we pack it in. Marching orders." His father laughed. Jeffery thought he knew what the laugh meant. It meant women. And men. Women and men to-gether. The accumulation. He was laughing at himself, at his life. Life with no escape. His father was a happy man. He was on vacation and this was his first act of recreation.

Once they'd filled in the old hole, Jeffery chose a good spot with loose soil and not too many roots to hack through. "I'll do it, Dad," he said, making the first cut by hopping up onto the spade with both feet. His father looked at him skeptically.

"Are you sure?"

"Yes, ab-so-tively."

"Leave moving the thing until the morning. Okay?"

"You bet."

His father thanked him and told him not to overdo it. It really didn't have to be done tonight, he said.

"I'll take it easy," said Jeffery, carving the edges of the new hole, tossing the sandy loam.

As he dug he seemed to gain energy, despite the mosquitoes and the sweat getting into his eyes. He felt inexhaustible. He felt exfoliated, newly poured and com-pacted, a foundling yet to be named and put to use in the world.

End of Play

The little girl reached up with her pudgy fingers to touch a pale crescent scar on Peter Levangie's cheek.

"Okay, spit."

"How come he doesn't talk?" she said looking over at a slim man sitting under a pot-bound spider plant by the window. He was dressed in tennis whites—long pants and V-neck sweater—and with his blond-crew cut, watery blue eyes and broad shoulders he looked like a sportswear model. His only physical flaw was a flattened nose, narrow at the bridge and widening downward with a twist like a vase that had been fired at too low a heat.

"He just likes to watch me work, honey."

"Did he already say everything he wanted to say?"

"I guess he did."

"What's his name? He looks far far away like a cloud."

"His name is KB and if you're really good while I do a little polishing maybe afterwards he'll give you a treat."

"What's he going to give me?"

"Something sugarless. A pony. Open wide, baby, that's a brave girl. You got lovely pearlies."

"Does KB have nice teeth, too?"

"Nice fake ones."

She wanted to ask what had happened, he could tell, but by then the polisher was buzzing and she closed her eyes against the overhead lamp and started humming an open-mouthed glottal tune in tandem with the sounds made by the cleaning tool and by the suction tube when it snagged the inside of her cheek.

KB had two tall stools he liked to sit on, one for each treatment-room Dr. Levangie maintained. In whichever room the doctor was working KB sat and watched. The dental assistant, Fanny Mallow, who had it in mind to marry Peter Levangie, thought KB an odd and unsettling addition to the office, although he had a calming effect on the more anxious patients. She had been working there only a few months when the doctor drove to Kingston and brought the strange handsome young man home with him. The first thing he did was fit him for a set of dentures.

According to Bev, the receptionist, who maintained the accounts, KB wasn't on the payroll, and she was pretty sure he lived with Dr. Levangie. "Simple in the head. Couldn't ever survive on his own. They had to give him the electroshock. That's why all his teeth fell out." Fanny couldn't imagine anyone so blanked out and peaceful being a threat to society.

At the end of the day the two men went out the door together, and, as he always did, KB ducked back in a minute later, reached behind one of the couches, retrieved a trophy about the size of a wine bottle, and placed it on the top shelf of the bookcase before going out again. A gold-coloured plate metal hockey player stood in the ready position with his stick blade on the ice. A name-plate identified the prize. Underneath was a gummy residue in the space where another plate had once been attached. Each morning as soon as he came in Dr. Levangie took the trophy down and returned it to its hiding place.

"Why do you two do that, play that hide-and-seek game?" she asked finally, after the hundredth time. "And who was Dirk Plomsky, if I may be so bold?"

"Dirk Plomsky was the man who loved ice hockey most of anyone in the world. Someday I'll tell you about him."

"I'm not going anywhere."

"That's good to hear," he said, thinking that with those words she had brought him a jump closer to a bigger intention, and he fingered the thought the way a man plays with the car keys in his pocket. He still treated her with a kind of surprised deference, as if she were a visiting dignitary who had arrived a day early. "I was wondering. Dinner. Eating must be on your...." Why was this so difficult?

He'd sooner have the graphite shaft of a Sherwood Special rammed crossways against his throat.

He took her to a Thai restaurant near Theatre Passe Muraille, where they had first met. She was an actress who needed a fall-back steady. Bev filled in when she was away, which wasn't that often, just long enough to make him miss her. After they'd ordered he asked her if she liked hockey and she said she'd never really thought about it.

"But I do want to hear about this Deke guy."

Dirk "Deke" Plomsky's claim to fame was that he had once played in an exhibition game in 1964 with Gordie Howe. He worked all his adult life until age 43 for Vectrolon, a Clayton auto-parts manufacturer. One day, not long after the last and worst game of his coaching career in minor hockey, Deke felt ill. He had just sent one of his fork-lift drivers away to bring forward a gross of solenoids, when he sat down hard on the corner of his desk. A Zamboni's weight was crushing the breath out of him, a freshly sharpened skate-blade slicing open the length of his left arm. He had time to scrawl across a blank requisition form:

I see Kanes Bartoe in super-white, hes a docter or an angel, whats the diff, hes so brite. If I go over make a trophee, in-grave it, and the 1st recip. shld bee

but by then the buzzer had sounded ending regulation play for Coach Plomsky.

The six players of the A-line were called into service as pallbearers, with Keynes Bartow and Peewee Levangie paired at the front end, the white coffin listing to Peewee's corner like a barge plunging into the trough of a mountainous wave. Every time he tried to lift and level out he felt the coach's bulk shift and bump toward Keynes. As in life, so in death, he thought. The shackles binding his legs kept Keynes' stride equal to Peewee's. After the interment the guards put the handcuffs on Deke Plomsky's dream player and drove him back to his cell to await trial.

Before that last harrowing game, Peewee pretty much despised Keynes Bartow and all he represented. Keynes played centre forward and spent most of the game drifting languidly around the midway red line the way a gigolo idles in a hotel lobby. He was a gorgeous long-strider evocative of Béliveau, proportional in face and body, effortless like a long-distance speed skater. He would ghost-train in on goal, lower his right shoulder, feign a move to the right to put the net-minder in irons, then stretch the poor Michelin man horizontal across the crease as he faded left and flipped the puck over a flailing outstretched trap. Or he might slap a heat-seeker from halfway between the blue line and the net, *la rondelle* never leaving the playing surface, the shot so quick it would clang off the goal's metal skirt and carom out before the defender had a chance to prepare.

All the mothers and sisters were in love with him with his plump lips and his sweater hitched up provocatively on one side. He knew how good he was and how pretty, but bore the knowledge naturally as if it were a facial birthmark he was no longer self-conscious about. Peewee had no time for him because Keynes didn't partake of the honest work, the stand-your-ground, the shots to the kidney, the noses giving way in floral bloom against Plexiglas. But what did it matter? Bartow knew where the puck was going to be in two seconds, seven seconds. The play would be ratcheting along in one direction like a marching band of the undead and he, he would be drifting with the nonchalance of the studied indolent in the opposite, careless, not even looking at the crunching mayhem when, click, he describes a tight curl, receives the disc on the blade of his stick the way the host is taken upon a faithful tongue, hesitates long enough to see the future, unconcerned that he is now the hunted, and sends the hard black pie out across open territory. No-one is there. It appears he has given it away at the expense of his patrician bust of a head, that never broken nose, those 32 pearls of piano-key uniformity. As if conjured there his right-winger arrives to find himself in possession and alone with a clear path, the remainder of the magic trick up to him, though he knows who is following up ready to sew closed this tidy scrap of sorcery. Or maybe not. Maybe the playmaker is so sure of his handiwork that he has turned his back on it. Maybe he is skating back to the team bench even before the transaction is completed. He might as well be a gymnast on the rings, the way he plays.

Talent scouts tried to convince Keynes to play Junior A, but he liked it wide open there in the lesser league, the checking comparatively lax and haphazard. He liked being able to take the play behind the opposing net and wait there for a few heartbeats, slowing the pace, or swoop in, around and out the other side, tucking the puck between the post and the goalie's foot. He scored goals the way his mother hooked her rugs, mindlessly, dexterously, always thinking of the finished product.

For someone with such a snooty sounding name, Keynes Bartow came from a poor family. His father was a Via Rail conductor who had never seen him play, his mother a Loblaws grocery clerk who came to the games when she had time off work, but who could hardly stand to watch. She would fasten her eyes on her son while he glided across the ice, casting a protective bubble around him, keeping him away from the muscle-tear corners and the shoulder-dislocating boards. When he was off the ice resting she closed her eyes against the uproar and hugged herself for warmth.

Millionaire paver Larry Levangie, on the other hand, his wet cigar perverting the shape of his mouth, bellowed and slapped the boards through all three periods of play. Fur-collared, full-length brown-leather coated, wearer of black Persian wool astrakhan, a bluejay-voiced man with outraged black caterpillars humped over his eyes, he rarely sat in the cold bleachers. Good play, bad play, what did he know about it? The thing to do was to make a glorious honk, because that was his boy holding the blue line there, smallest prick on the ice, scrappiest, permanent resident of the corners after hard rubber, his body a grader, a front-end loader. Larry gave him $100 a goal and $50 for every shot blocked. The boy already had four gold crowns replacing teeth he'd sacrificed to the game.

But defenceman Peewee Levangie didn't care about the cash, and he wanted something more than the top plus-minus average, which he had already achieved, more than the scoring title, which he had missed by two assists, more than a league championship or his name in the newspaper. As soon as he heard about it after the coach croaked, and because he had a good idea who the first recipient was going to be, he coveted the Dirk Plomsky Memorial Trophy, named for the Pekinese-dog-faced man who had no children of his own, a man so fiercely in love with his players that at times they were afraid he was going to latch onto their soft tissue with his snarling snout and rip them open in appreciation of the game. Peewee wanted his father to see him win the prize old Deke himself would have bestowed on one of his surrogate sons. He wanted it for what he had done but couldn't tell anyone about. It was hopeless.

The trophy, they decided, the assistant coach and Plomsky's widow and some other boosters who were fairly neutral on the question, would go to the player who best personified those qualities of leadership and passion most evocative of the late coach. No-one was surprised when they gave it to Keynes in absentia, not that the honour registered in what was left of the winner's mind. A leader? Peewee wanted to ask. Out there in a holding pattern in the sissy zone, unhelpful in the clinches, slow coming back after a rush? He never used his body to stop an opponent, occasionally poking or sweeping with his long stick, flicking it out and snagging the puck as if he were fencing or fly-fishing. The prissy deviousness of it, the practiced artifice. Why didn't the faggot just go arrange flowers and leave the game to those, like him, who cared with their guts, who played the body first, the puck second? But these were uncharitable thoughts, given all that had happened.

Peewee blamed it all on the final game of their most recent tournament, in Saint Lazare, P.Q. They, the Vectrolon Heat, were battling a team from Labrador for third place in the consolation round. The local girls took one look at Keynes and became his swooning, ever-to-the-death devoted fan club, a dozen sweet chanteuses who tried to imagine what his head looked like. They waved their hand-warmers and scarves at him in an effort to make him smile. They conspired with members of the other team to draw him into a fight so that they might visit him in the penalty box, but he refused to be enticed into fisticuffs, even in the last minute of the game when the Labradors, losing 4 to 2 after a Bartow lob into their open net, dropped their gloves. Both benches emptied and they all found partners like sweaty spastics at their first social mixer. Gladiatorial helmets flew off revealing hot mats of wet hair. Exposed skin and a musky male tang delighted the chanteuses. It was early in the new day and this beat anything *la rue principale* had to offer that night.

Mr. Levangie was apoplectic with joy as he reached across the chest-high wall. He wanted in. His son was up against his own team's bench for support and leverage, the way he had taught him, paired with a towering aboriginal person who had huge thighs and the smell of fish oil on him. Peewee had the Innu boy's sweater pulled over his face and was holding him with his left hand while he gut-punched him with his right. It resembled a disembowelment. The boy didn't want to fight; he just did what his mates were doing, what his coach exhorted him to do, this thuggery, this venting of bad humour. Peewee couldn't put him down, just kept digging into the foam-rubber muskeg of his mid-section until he tired, hardly able to lift his hand to strike. The snowmobile jockey of broad face and noble bone structure stood rooted as he pushed down on Peewee's head to hold him in abeyance. The black-and-white striped referees let it happen by making a quick exit of the rink. Parents came out onto the ice surface, either to fight or to save their sons, and they fell, cracking elbows and hipbones in a *mêlée* of up and down. The clock had run out. The arena manager turned out the lights in an effort to halt the rumble, but it continued of its own momentum, fuelled by spunk and uppers, caffeine and steroids, sugar and testosterone, Mummy with her eyes jammed shut and Daddy breaking his knuckles on the draped head of the nanook whose name was Bertram Alootook and who could have rendered father and son quadriplegics in a single clasp. It was becoming a spent, tedious thing, this brawl in the dark, like the final minutes of a month-long dance marathon. Boys, bleeding, spat out their teeth and hung onto each other in their revealed armour. The chanteuses knew the shape of Keynes Bartow's head and moaned for more, his shoulders, his chest, his bare arms. They touched themselves through their layers in the dark cold. The ice-cleaning machine came out, the driver yelling at them to *Vas-y!* lest he turn them into flattened decals pressed into *la glace*, and so, sheepish, blunted of purpose, not yet feeling their bruises, they skated around, blind in the headlight glare of the water-closet on wheels, in a meandering retrieval of paraphernalia.

When he finally saw Bertram Alootook's face, after breaking free for a time in the dark and coming back, Peewee saw nothing but fellow feeling in the boy's eyes, no hurt, no anger or hatred, and he was bewildered by it. He had the boy's nose blood in his hair. He had blood on his skate-blades. He looked over at the team bench. The headlight lit Keynes' face for an instant. He was sitting leaning back with his head tilted up and his eyes closed, Coach Plomsky holding a cold pack to the side of his face. Not his mother, not Hork Fenestra, the equipment boy, but Deke himself, and the look on the man's face, the love, the awe, it stopped Peewee dead with wonder, made him sick to witness.

In the dressing-room they sat barely able to move. No-one could remember the game, its outcome. In the middle of the floor lay heaped a pile of equipment that had been salvaged from the ice. As they stripped they threw their shoulder pads, elbow pads, padded pants, cups, jockstraps, helmets, mouthguards, hockey sticks, spare rolls of white surgical tape, not into their duffel bags but onto the pile. "Burn it," said Hork's big brother, Gob, and others concurred. Douse it, light it now, light up my bruised cheeks, my split lips with it. This life it is over. I am now a man, whatever that is. I am spent of boisterousness. It is the end of play. This requires a ceremony of termination. Let us bury our dead selves.

Peewee wiped his skates carefully with a damp rag, then used it on Keynes' blades. He stowed his pads in his bag. "What's all this foolishness?" he said. "There'll be other games, guys." He was going to be a counsellor at a summer hockey camp up in Haileybury. The Great One was going to make an appearance, it was rumoured. Junior A was only a few months of Howie Meeker power skating and weight-work away.

"You didn't see?"

"See what?"

"How could you not have seen? You were out there."

"I'm industrious. I keep focus."

It began when Keynes scored the clincher and the out-landers saw their hopes for overtime slip down the oil-slicked rocks of disappointment. Their captain, 66, a flashy little Middle-Eastern-looking player, got it in his eyes and fists to take out his bereavement on Keynes. Deke could see the agenda hand-stitched on the back of the kid's jersey. "You can't tell me there's no mischief in that. You all saw it. Where were you, Levangie, were you blowing that big Tuk?"

The Arab-devil didn't even wait until the buzzer had sounded. He scanned the expanse of frozen water as if looking for a breathing hole, and spied his intended victim. He cut the golden boy off, slashing his stick out of his hands. That it should sink so low, to this, to lamentable stick work. The next blow, glancing from the side, neatly removed Keynes' helmet. The next, a lord high executioner chop from the rafters came down squarely, the heel sinking, it seemed, with a dull thud into the top back of the skull and he went down, pole-axed, an abattoir steer. Blink One: upright, skating toward his bench; Blink Two: down, a loose sack of crushed stone dropped from a roof. Flat, face first, nose broken cleanly and pushed to one side. The unison gasp as they waited, hoping for more but nauseous from the expectation of it, with a voice from inside saying, Stop this do something remove all weapons from the hands of our children hit him again. Oh, my life, somebody hit!

Keynes got wobbly to his feet. He started skating in the wrong direction, away from his bench and toward the penalty box across the ice, not sure where he was. His attacker followed him, used his stick again, this time to trip him. Keynes fell face-down again, a red halo spreading. The bastard was now kneeling on his quarry's back and pummelling with his bare knuckles. The lights went out.

The Zamboni wasn't on the ice yet. They weren't sure that what they had seen had happened. Mrs. Bartow was on her feet, yelling, "Stop it! Stop the barbarity! My son is hurt out there!" Who could say in the pitch black dark what cruelty was being perpetrated upon Keynes Bartow, the prettiest, the sweetest? Everyone was drowning.

With only one person knowing when it happened or how, Keynes was back on his bench, and Coach Deke him-

146

self attended to the destroyed nose, the cracked cheekbone, the gushing scalp wound. "Lean back, lean back into my healing arms, son." Those who were close enough, for an instant in the headlight glare, saw a strange *pietà* in the aftermath: a noseless little dog-faced man made beautiful in his devotion as he cradled the head of his anointed one, who hadn't fought. Who'd got to his feet repeatedly with wood and bone raining down upon his neck and crown. Stupidly he'd skated away, a naïf, a cheek-turner.

Peewee looked over at Keynes, whose mouth gaped open. Wads of dripping gauze were stuck up his nostrils. Hork Fenestra was struggling to help him remove his equipment, saying, "Which are yours, is this your shirt? Lift your arm a sec." The eyes were not quite focused, both gross and fine motor skills down by half.

Because there was nowhere else to go so early on a Sunday morning except back to the motel where they were staying and because they didn't feel like sleeping, they crowded into the Emergency waiting-room of the Hôtel Dieu. The doctor came out and told them it was too early to tell, but there could be some brain damage. She was going to give Keynes a drug to reduce the swelling around his brain and prevent seizures, and keep him overnight for observation.

Mrs. Bartow stayed the night with her son, who had not said a word since the attack. Mr. Levangie stayed, too, to comfort her, getting her cup after cup of coffee from a vending machine. He told his son to go back to the motel. "I'd rather stay," said Peewee, and his father grunted, "Suit yourself." So the three of them sat vigil around the bed as Keynes slipped in and out of consciousness.

The coach came back around six in the morning accompanied by two burly Sûreté du Québec officers who wanted to question Keynes because the boy who had attacked him had been found dead, stuffed under the bench in the penalty box, his throat slit open. They had found blood on one of Keynes' skate-blades and on a rag in his equipment bag.

"He may never wake up," said Deke, hopefully.

"Oh, he will wake up for this, monsieur," said one of the officers.

Pete Levangie played two years with the 67s and then four with the Leafs before a recurring back injury forced him to quit. He wasn't unhappy about the decision, never feeling that hockey was all there was to his life. During his career as a fearless and diligent defenceman he travelled widely and saved his money. He saw many of his teammates and opponents lose their teeth to the game, and so when he retired he went to university and put in the years of study necessary to become a dental surgeon. He was particularly good with children because he was short and had a youthful face, a happy face as the little girl called it while he was leaning over her. He *was* a happy man. He did good work. He was in love. He hoped that Fanny Mallow would say yes and continue to say yes for the rest of their lives together. He hoped she wouldn't mind living with two ageing athletes instead of just one.

His patient reached up through his dreaming to touch his face with her sticky fingers, bringing him back to the work at hand.

"We all start out harmless," he said, gently scraping, testing with a nasty-looking pick. But she wasn't listening. She was stretching her eyes to the edge of their sockets to keep the shining man in her field of vision.